Danger

Annie had a strong impulse to burst out of the hatch and tell Señor Bernabo what she thought of him, but a feeling of caution stopped her. She wondered what he was doing here at the castle and what the argument was all about.

After a few more minutes, the pair moved away, and the room became silent once more.

'D'you think it's safe to go up now?' whispered Pip.

'Cross your fingers we can get the hatch open!' said Annie.

She and Cherry found a ring in the wood panel and pulled hard, but it wouldn't budge.

'Oh, no!' groaned Pip. 'Don't say we're stuck here!'

Annie was feeling all round the panel blindly. 'There must be a way of opening it from this side,' she said, trying not to panic.

More footsteps echoed through their hiding-place, and they were forced to stay still once more. This time, it probably was an attendant, as the footsteps did a tour of the room and then departed.

'Oh hurry up and get us out!' gasped Pip. 'I feel as if I'm suffocating!'

'I'm doing my best,' said Annie, using her fingers as eyes once more.

THE DANCE CLUB
SERIES

DANCE CLUB

4

DANGER
AT THE
CASTLE

•

Mal Lewis Jones

MACDONALD YOUNG BOOKS

Text copyright © Mal Lewis Jones 1996

First published in Great Britain in 1996
by Macdonald Young Books
61 Western Road
Hove
East Sussex
BN3 1JD

Photoset in North Wales by
Derek Doyle & Associates, Mold, Clwyd.
Printed and bound in Great Britain by
The Guernsey Press Co. Ltd., Guernsey, Channel Islands

British Library Cataloguing in Publication Data available.

ISBN: 0 7500 1962 X
ISBN: 0 7500 2136 5 (pb)

Contents

A Night in the Tower

Annie Macdonald woke with a start, and then lay back in the big four-poster bed, remembering where she was. She was spending the last few days of the Easter holiday at her friend's castle. Pip Williams – whose home was Totley Castle – had also invited their other friend from the Dance Club, Cherry Stevens.

The three girls had spent a wonderful couple of days swimming, riding and dancing together. But Pip had saved up a special treat for her friends' last day, which was today.

The Tower was going to be reopened, after full restoration. Pip's parents had promised that the girls could be the first to stay in it. They were going to make their own meals, and sleep in the Tower for their last night.

Annie felt very excited about it, and a little apprehensive too. On a previous visit to Totley, she had been trapped in the Tower in the dark, and had been badly frightened. But Pip assured her that now it had been refurbished, and had the electricity working once more, it had a very different kind of atmosphere.

Annie dressed quickly. Even though it was early April, the nights and early mornings were still cold. She went across to Cherry's room, to see if she was awake, but Cherry was still fast asleep. When she tiptoed into Pip's room, Pip stirred and sat up.

'Hello,' said Pip. 'You're up early.'

'I was too excited to sleep,' Annie said, plopping herself down on Pip's bed.

'Ouch! Watch my feet!' yelled Pip.

'Oh sorry,' Annie apologized.

'About the Tower?' asked Pip.

'What about the Tower?' asked Annie.

'Getting excited, I mean,' said Pip.

'Aye,' said Annie. 'I can't wait. I can hardly believe it will have running water and electric lights and everything.' Her mind flew back to how the Tower had looked before renovation – sombre, mysterious, half-crumbling, cobwebby.

'It's going to be as much of a surprise for me as for you!' cried Pip. 'Daddy hasn't let me set foot inside it while the builders have been in.'

'Shall we wake Cherry?' asked Annie.

'No, better let her sleep a bit longer,' said Pip. 'I'll get up now though. We can go down and have an early breakfast.'

Mrs Williams was not yet up, but the girls sat down to breakfast in the large country-style kitchen with Pip's father.

'Tuck in, Annie,' he urged her, in his American drawl. 'This might be your last square meal of the day!' He chuckled before finishing his last piece of toast and marmalade.

'Oh Dad,' said Pip. 'We can cook as well as you can. We're certainly not going to starve, are we Annie?'

'Not by the look of the box of food you've packed for us, no,' said Annie, laughing.

'I bet Pip's looking forward to showing you the Tower,' said Mr Williams. 'We haven't been able to let visitors in for years. It's been far too dangerous.'

Annie nodded, feeling guilty. She had made two visits to the Tower without Pip's parents' knowledge. But then she remembered that if she hadn't she wouldn't have found the will. This was at a time when repairs to the main castle had proved so expensive that the family thought they would have to sell it. Eliza Sandown's will, however, had enabled the Williamses to pay for the repairs and to stay at Totley.

'It'll be a good opportunity for you to see it,' said Pip's dad. 'We're going to let it out through a tourism agency, so I guess it will be occupied by guests for a good deal of the year, once it gets started.'

'Oh that's a great idea,' said Annie. 'It'll give lots of people the chance to enjoy Totley.'

'Without getting under our feet,' Pip added.

Mr Williams excused himself, as he had to get ready for work. The girls went back upstairs and woke Cherry up.

'Oh, it's you,' she said, rubbing her eyes. 'I was having such a lovely dream.'

'Come on, Cherry, get up,' Annie said impatiently. 'We're moving into the Tower today, remember?'

Annie was staggered by the change which had come over the place. When she opened the great oak door and walked in, her feet sank into luxurious, mushroom-coloured carpet. The ground floor had been divided up into a fully-fitted kitchen, with oak cupboards, and a dining-room with an oak gateleg table and chairs with legs that looked like twisty sticks of barley sugar. The walls were freshly painted. There was no trace of dust or cobweb anywhere.

'It's amazing!' Annie said.

'Let's go upstairs,' said Pip. 'I had no idea it would look *so* different.'

The once crumbling spiral staircase had been made safe. They trooped up it to the first floor, which provided a large circular sitting-room, very comfortably furnished.

'This will make a great holiday home,' said Cherry.

The next two floors provided bedrooms, and the girls decided to share the very top one. There was no shortage of beds. In this room alone there was a double bed and a pair of bunk beds.

'I can't believe this is the same room I was trapped in!' Annie declared, testing the double bed, and looking at the colourful new bedspreads and curtains.

'Yes, no more funny noises either,' said Pip. 'We got rid of the mice.'

'Poor things,' said Annie. 'I wonder where they went.'

'It's spring now anyway,' said Pip. 'They only usually come indoors during the winter.'

While Annie thought the Tower had been beautifully renovated, she still felt a little sad at the changes. A lot of its mystery and romance had gone for ever, in her view.

On the other hand, it was going to be tremendous fun living in the Tower on their own.

In actual fact, they had several visits from Pip's mother and even Bob, who was the family's Jack-of-all-trades, during the day and evening, to check they were coping with the cooking, and had turned everything off after they'd finished.

Once they'd sat down to their evening meal, however, they knew they'd be left alone till morning. Together they had prepared cheese and potato pie, carrots, and peas, with fresh fruit and ice-cream for afters.

'That feels better,' sighed Annie pushing her

empty dish to one side.

'Haven't you got room for a doughnut?' asked Pip, smiling.

'Course I have,' said Annie.

'And me,' said Cherry, hopefully.

Pip had smuggled in a pack of four. 'Who's going to have the odd one?' she said.

'The ghost!' said Cherry, laughing.

Annie felt able to laugh with her now. She no longer felt that the Tower was haunted.

'We'll share it,' said Annie.

'I guess you've had enough of ghosts for a while,' said Pip.

'Quite enough,' said Annie.

'You were really taken in, weren't you?' said Cherry.

'So were you,' Annie retorted, 'by the skeleton at least.'

Cherry opened her mouth to argue, but thought better of it. 'Yes, I admit, I was frightened of Fred at first. He just caught me unawares, that's all!'

Pip grinned at her. 'You screamed your head off,' she said.

'So did you!' said Cherry.

'Well, we all suffered from Maria's pranks,' said Annie. 'Thank goodness we found out she was behind it all.'

'Yes, and we won't have the pleasure of Maria's company at Dance Club this term,' said Pip.

'It'll be heaven,' said Cherry.

'Zoë's left too,' said Annie. 'Our numbers will be

down a bit!'

'Never mind,' said Cherry. 'It's the kind of people who are in the club that matter, not how many.'

'I suppose you're dying to start a new piece for a show or something,' said Pip.

'It would be nice,' said Annie, nodding, 'if we got the opportunity.'

'Are you looking forward to going back to school?' asked Cherry.

'Sort of,' said Annie, 'though we've had such a good time here, it'll be a bit hard to leave.'

'I feel the same,' said Cherry.

'Just think, the day after tomorrow the exchange students are arriving!'

A party of girls and boys from Spain were coming to stay in Shropshire, as part of an exchange programme run by Bishop's School.

'Oh, I'd forgotten it was so soon,' Annie exclaimed. 'We've got to meet them off their coach at school, haven't we?'

'That's right,' said Pip.

'I bet yours will have a shock when they see the castle!' said Annie. Pip was going to put up two of the girls and a female teacher.

'I'm glad I'm only having one Spanish girl,' said Cherry. 'I don't think I could cope with two.'

'I think it might be easier with two though,' said Pip, 'because they can talk to each other. You're having two, aren't you, Annie?'

'Nay, only one girl – Gina, I think her name is. But we're having her uncle to stay as well.'

'That's funny, isn't it?' remarked Cherry. 'I didn't think there were any parents or relatives coming with them, just teachers.'

'He's the only one, I think,' said Annie. 'I heard Mr Reynolds saying something to Dad about him wanting to do some research into historic buildings in Shropshire.'

'He ought to have been placed here, really!' said Pip.

'That would have made sense,' Annie said. 'Anyway, I just hope we all get on with our Spanish visitors.'

'How long are they here for?' said Cherry.

'Three weeks!' Annie exclaimed. 'It'll seem ages. I bet I don't get on with mine!'

'Don't be silly,' said Cherry, 'you haven't even met them yet!'

'I know,' said Annie, 'but I've just got a funny feeling about this Gina and her uncle.'

· 2 ·

A Surprise for Robbie

Once she was back at school the next day, Annie realized how much the Easter holiday had refreshed her. The pressures of the show and her ballet exam behind her, she looked forward to a more relaxed summer term.

She hadn't managed to see her new friend Clemmie over the holiday. Clemmie and her family had gone back to Canterbury to stay with relatives for Easter. Annie was looking forward to hearing her news. She found her in the girls' cloakroom before lessons.

'Hi, Clemmie! Had a good holiday?'

'Oh hello, Annie,' Clemmie replied. Now that

Annie was closer, she could see Clemmie didn't look happy.

'What's the matter?' asked Annie.

'Nothing,' said Clemmie, hunching her shoulders.

'Come on, Clemmie!' cried Annie. 'You can talk to me, remember!'

This seemed to make Clemmie snap out of her mood. 'Sorry, Annie,' she said. 'It seems such a long time since I had a chat with you, I'd almost forgotten what it's like to talk freely.'

'So what's wrong?' asked Annie. 'Didn't you enjoy going back to Canterbury?'

Before Clemmie could answer, a crowd of other girls came bursting into the cloakroom, Cherry and Pip among them.

'Hi, Annie – Hi, Clemmie!' they chorused.

'I'll tell you later,' Clemmie whispered to Annie. Annie was quickly caught up in an excited hubbub with her other friends, but she felt curious about what had upset Clemmie, and hoped it wasn't anything too awful.

Clemmie had found it so difficult settling in at Bishop's at the start of the previous term. Annie had done everything she could to boost Clemmie's confidence.

By the end of term, it seemed to have worked – Clemmie was doing very well in her academic work and had shown a flair for dressmaking, which came in very useful for Miss Rodelle's show. But most important of all, she was much more at ease with her classmates. Annie hoped that she hadn't taken a backward step over the holiday.

As the girls made their way to their form room, Sam and Robbie caught them up.

'Getting excited?' asked Sam.

'Should we be?' Pip replied with a smile.

Annie wondered if he was going to ask Pip for another date, and began to feel flustered, in case Robbie asked her.

'About the Spanish students!' Sam explained. 'We'll meet them tonight.'

It turned out that Sam and Robbie were each going to look after a Spanish boy.

'I'm looking forward to all the outings,' said Robbie, smiling. Annie allowed herself a quick glance at his face. She loved his smile. Then she quickly looked away again.

'We don't get to go on any!' cried Sam. 'Whatever made you think we did? It's just for the visitors.'

Robbie turned a bit pink, and Annie felt very sorry for him – she searched her mind for something to say, to make him feel better, but could think of nothing.

'I'm looking forward to our return visit,' she said at last. 'I've never been to Spain. And then it'll be our turn to go on outings.'

She smiled at Robbie reassuringly, but noticed, with alarm, that he looked more embarrassed than ever. Muttering an excuse, Robbie left the group and hurried on ahead.

'Did I say the wrong thing?' asked Annie, feeling worried.

'Probably,' said Sam breezily. 'But don't worry, he'll be all right. Just a bit touchy about the Spanish exchange, that's all.'

'But why?' asked Annie.

'Because he can't afford to go to Spain after all,' Sam replied. 'His dad's just lost his job.'

'Oh,' said Annie, feeling worse than ever. If only she'd known this before she'd said anything.

'Trust me to put my foot in it,' she said to Cherry and Pip, when Sam had gone.

'It wasn't your fault,' said Cherry. 'There are going to be a lot of other people talking about the visit to Spain.'

'I still feel awful,' said Annie. 'I always seem to do the wrong thing where Robbie's concerned.'

By an unfortunate coincidence, their very first lesson was Spanish.

'Buenos días,' Mrs Ellis greeted them. She was a petite blonde woman in her mid thirties, with a rather sharp manner. 'As we are expecting our visitors tonight, I thought I would spend part of the lesson talking to you about the Spanish town they come from, as the majority of you will be making the return visit there in October.'

Annie glanced over at Robbie. He was looking very uncomfortable. She guessed suddenly that he hadn't yet spoken to Mrs Ellis about cancelling his trip to Spain.

Her eyes moved to Clemmie. She still looked miserable, and Annie again wondered what the problem was.

Her attention came back to Mrs Ellis's descriptions of the Spanish town:

'Torrevieja is a large, bustling town with a busy port and an important salt-extraction works,' she said. 'It is on the south-east coast of Spain. Let's see if anyone can tell me what the name means? Split it up into two – torre and vieja.'

Sam put up his hand. 'Is it something to do with bullfighting?'

'No,' said Mrs Ellis irritably. 'You're thinking of *toro*, which means bull.'

Sam sank into his seat, as Maria put up her hand.

'Yes, Maria?'

'Torre means tower, doesn't it? So Torrevieja must mean Old Tower,' Maria said smugly.

'Quite right, Maria,' said Mrs Ellis. 'I'm glad to see *someone* is remembering her vocabulary.'

Pip nudged Annie in the ribs. 'Funny it should be called Old Tower!'

Annie gave her a warning frown, as Mrs Ellis's eagle eye swooped down on them.

'When you've finished chattering, I'll continue,' she said. 'You'll be pleased to hear that there is a lovely beach running alongside the town. The temperature will still be hot enough to do some swimming, I dare say.'

'I can't wait, can you?' Cherry whispered.

'Sounds lovely,' Annie whispered back. 'But what if we don't get on with our student? Staying with someone you didn't like wouldn't be much fun, would it?'

'What are you whispering about, Annie Macdonald?' Mrs Ellis asked suddenly. 'Would you like to share your comments with the rest of us?'

Annie blushed. 'Er, I was just saying to Cherry that – er – it wouldn't be much fun staying with someone you didn't like.'

'That's a very negative remark,' said Mrs Ellis, sounding a bit cross. 'If you meet your student in that frame of mind, I can imagine what will happen. Let me impress upon you all these are Year Eight pupils, just like you. You all manage to get on together well, don't you?'

There was a general murmur of assent from round the classroom. Annie looked over at Maria doubtfully.

'The only difference,' continued Mrs Ellis, 'is that these youngsters are Spanish. They have all been learning English from their Primary school days – a lot longer than you.'

Indeed, the class had only been taking Spanish lessons for two terms.

'You'll find they'll be able to converse with you reasonably well, as long as you remember to keep what you say simple and clear. Be good hosts to them, please. They're visiting a foreign country, most of them for the first time. Give them a warm welcome and a good time and I'm sure you will get the same treatment when you make your return visit.'

By the end of the lesson, Annie was feeling more, rather than less, anxious about her Spanish visitor.

Pip was having misgivings too.

'I've had a horrible thought!' she announced. 'You know we've got the Spanish teacher staying with us. Well, when we go over there, what if I have to stay in the same house as Mrs Ellis!'

Pip looked so aghast, that her friends couldn't help laughing at her.

'Well, she's got to stay with someone!' said Cherry, giggling.

'I just hope it's not me,' wailed Pip.

'She's not so bad really,' said Cherry. 'She just can't understand why other people don't love Spain as much as she does!'

'She made me feel really small,' said Annie.

'She wasn't very nice to Sam either,' Pip added.

Annie looked round at the milling students in the corridor, hoping to catch sight of Clemmie, but she couldn't spot her.

It wasn't until morning break that Annie had a chance to speak to her privately. Clemmie had seemed very quiet all morning.

'What's bothering you?' asked Annie.

'There's nothing much to tell you,' said Clemmie, shrugging. 'I just lost my confidence a bit over the holiday, that's all.'

'Did you have trouble coming to school this morning?' Annie asked sympathetically.

'Yes, I was dreading it,' Clemmie admitted, 'but I feel a bit better now.'

'Make sure you come to Dance Club at lunch-time,' said Annie. 'We can't have you moping around on your own.'

'OK.' said Clemmie. 'D'you still want me to be in charge of the cassette player?'

'Of course,' said Annie, 'and, just as soon as we're involved in a show again, I want you to be our costume designer.'

Clemmie's pale skin was lit by a rosy glow. 'Thanks Annie,' she said.

Annie felt relieved that Clemmie seemed all right. She threw herself whole-heartedly into leading the members of the Dance Club in a classical ballet class.

Once everyone had caught hold of a rung of a wall ladder to use as a barre, she took them through the basic pliés, battements and ronds de jambe that are every dancer's staple exercise.

As she got on to the more advanced exercises, there were the usual groans from club members who hadn't been practising over Easter.

'Slow down, Annie!' Robbie called out, at one point.

Annie didn't know whether to be pleased or not. At least he was speaking to her, but she wondered if he thought her hard-hearted.

During the afternoon, Annie thought quite a lot about Robbie. What did he think of her? Would there be any chance this term of getting to know him better?

In the spare moments between lessons, she was caught up in excited chatter with Pip and Cherry about the arrival of the Spanish students.

It wasn't until the very end of school that she noticed Clemmie again. With a pang, she realized she was looking lonely and 'out of it' once more. Eager to make up for her neglect, Annie rushed across.

'Clemmie!' she cried. 'I've been meaning to ask you all day. Would you like to come to my house after school tomorrow?'

Clemmie looked at her carefully. 'The Spanish students ...' she began.

'Oh that doesn't matter!' cried Annie, brushing away any possible obstacles. 'Mum won't mind a bit!'

'No, I'm sorry, I can't make it,' said Clemmie unexpectedly abrupt in her refusal.

Afterwards, when Annie thought about it, she wondered if Clemmie thought it would be rude to leave her own visitor.

'But why didn't she just say so?' Annie mused. No, Clemmie was behaving strangely again. And Annie no longer believed the explanation she had been given.

Annie barely had time to eat her tea before she was back again at school, this time with her family. They waited, along with dozens of other families, for the coach from Spain to arrive.

She found Cherry and Pip among the crowd.

'They're late, aren't they?' said Pip, looking at her watch.

'Perhaps the ferry crossing was delayed or something,' said Cherry.

'Have you seen Clemmie anywhere?' asked Annie, peering around.

'Was she having a student?' asked Pip.

'I thought we all were,' Annie replied.

'So did I,' said Cherry, 'unless Robbie has pulled out because he's not going to Spain.'

'No, he hasn't,' said Pip. 'According to Sam, Robbie's still having a Spanish boy to stay.'

'Clemmie seemed a bit odd today,' Annie remarked, still looking round for her.

'You mean odder than usual,' Cherry laughed.

'Don't be mean,' said Annie. 'She's one of us now.'

'Sorry,' Cherry apologized meekly.

At last, the coach arrived, and a rather tired and bedraggled-looking party stepped off it. Pip was the first to meet up with her visitors – the two girls looked nice enough, but the teacher looked bad-tempered.

'Good luck,' Annie whispered in her friend's ear before Pip guided her small party back to her father's waiting Range Rover.

'I'd love to see their faces when they get to the castle!' Annie said, laughing.

Cherry was called forward then by Mrs Ellis, to greet her student, whose name was Anita. What struck Annie straight away was that Anita had long red hair, like Cherry. *Well-matched*, she thought to herself. Her attention was drawn from Cherry and Anita by raised voices, which she identified as coming from behind the coach. She went to investigate. Robbie was standing, talking rapidly and loudly with Mrs Ellis, his mother and a small group of Spanish kids, plus a teacher.

'What's going on?' asked Annie. Everyone seemed rather excited.

Robbie looked embarrassed. 'You'll never guess, Annie,' he said, with a note of apology in his voice. 'I was expecting an *Antonio* to come and stay. That's the name that was written down on our letters. But well, *he* turns out to be *Antonia*!'

Annie followed the direction of his gaze. A very pretty girl with waist-length black hair was standing next to her teacher, looking as embarrassed as Robbie.

'I'm afraid we can't do anything about it just yet,' Mrs Ellis was saying to the Spanish teacher. 'Antonia will just have to manage at Robbie's until we can make other arrangements.'

Robbie pulled a face at Annie, as if to say it was the last thing he wanted, but Annie had seen a considerable interest in his eyes when he had been looking at the Spanish girl he was about to take home with him.

Her heart sank, as she moved once more towards the coach door. She suddenly realized that she was the last Bishop's pupil waiting. Her mother and Louisa came up to her.

'What's happened to our visitors then?' asked Mrs Macdonald.

'Perhaps they decided not to come,' Louisa said hopefully.

As they watched, the two very last travellers emerged from the coach.

'These must be ours,' Annie whispered.

There was a small, slightly stooped middle-aged man accompanied by a strikingly pretty, dark-haired girl.

Whereas most of the other girls and boys had got out of the coach looking crumpled and travel-stained, this girl looked fresh as a daisy. She was very dressed up, in a smart skirt and blouse and the sort of little-heeled court shoes that Annie's mum sometimes wore.

She smiled dazzlingly at Annie, as Mrs Ellis introduced them.

'Annie, Mrs Macdonald – this is Gina and her uncle, Señor Bernabo.'

· 3 ·

An Invitation from the Mayor

If she were honest with herself, Annie's first reaction to Gina Bernabo was one of dislike. This was despite Gina's winning smiles and effusive manner. She spoke English extremely well. Annie could hardly believe she had never set foot in Britain before.

Gina looked and dressed like a fifteen-year-old. Annie felt a mixture of envy and inferiority. Beside Gina, she felt like a plain little girl.

The rest of the family were bowled over by their charming and beautiful visitor. Mr Macdonald, in particular, sparkled at mealtimes, in contrast with his usual rather serious manner.

Even Louisa fell under Gina's spell, especially

when Gina began showing the younger girl her jewellery and make-up. Annie had little of either with which to impress Louisa, apart from her grease-paint, which was quite unpleasant to use. She felt her bedroom – which she had to share with Gina – had been taken over by an avalanche of femininity.

Señor Bernabo, by contrast, kept to his room (the small spare room) in the evenings, and was out all day doing his 'research'. The family only saw him at mealtimes and even then, he was silent and rather morose. He seemed to know very little English.

Annie would have expected Gina to be more helpful, translating some of the conversations that were going on around him, but she didn't seem to bother with him much at all.

Annie tried to say as much to her parents at the weekend, when Gina and her uncle were both out on a sightseeing trip organized by Mrs Ellis.

'He's a very reserved man, Señor Bernabo,' said her mother by way of reply.

'Aye, I don't suppose he really wants to understand all your chatter,' Mr Macdonald chipped in.

'I don't like him,' Annie said impulsively. She was feeling annoyed that her parents wouldn't agree with her that there was something lacking in Gina.

'You mustn't say things like that, dear,' said her mum with a reproving glance. 'He's a very nice gentleman, just a little quiet that's all.'

'Gina makes up for him, anyway,' said her father,

with a smile. 'Isn't her command of the English language excellent?'

Before she had to hear any further praise of Gina, Annie scooted off to her room. Only it didn't feel like her room any more. On every surface – normally neat and well-organized – were strewn hairbrushes, spray, gel, shampoo, conditioner, body lotion, body scrub, cleansing cream and many items of make-up and jewellery.

Annie sighed and sat on her bed. She put her head in her hands. She wouldn't know where to begin to tidy up. And Gina might not appreciate it, anyway. She often did her homework at the small desk in her bedroom, but now there was not a free inch of space on its surface.

She would have to go downstairs and use the kitchen table. She sighed again and sat where she was. Perhaps she was being really unfair. Gina was just different from her, that was all.

Her mum came into the room. 'Everything all right?' she asked.

'Sort of,' said Annie, 'but just look at this mess!'

'Don't worry,' said her mum. 'You'll soon be back to normal again. Aren't you enjoying having Gina to stay?'

'Not a lot,' said Annie. 'We're not really on the same wavelength.'

'You could try to make a bit more effort, you know,' said her mum. 'Gina's been trying really hard to be friendly to you, I've been noticing. But you haven't responded to her.'

'You're probably right,' said Annie. 'I'm sorry.'

When Gina came back, Annie made a special effort to chat to her. She asked her about her day, and answered all her questions about Shrewsbury.

'I'm glad I am staying near the town,' said Gina. 'Some of my friends – they go far away from Shrewsbury.'

Annie looked at her watch. 'Would you like to nip into town now? There's still an hour before the shops close.'

'Yes please!' exclaimed Gina.

In ten minutes, they were in the centre of Shrewsbury. Gina made a bee-line for a big department store and quickly found the teenage fashion section. Annie enjoyed browsing through the racks of clothes – it was something she rarely did. But after fifteen minutes or so, she'd had enough. She asked Gina if she'd finished looking, but Gina had no intention of leaving just yet. She tried on several different outfits in the changing rooms, asking Annie her opinion on each one.

By the sixth or seventh, Annie was desperate to go. 'Do you like this one best?' asked Gina, parading up and down the changing room, to the amusement of several other young women.

'Oh I don't know,' sighed Annie. 'Do you have to buy something today?'

Gina pouted. 'I want to get clothes from Shrewsbury. To show my family. But if you don't like …'

'It's not up to me,' Annie cut in. 'It's what you like

24

that's important.'

Gina studied herself in the mirror. 'I think the first one was the best,' she said.

Ripping off the latest outfit, she found the first dress she had tried, and put it on once more. 'Olé!' she cried, doing a twirl.

Annie couldn't wait to get out of the store. Nothing would tempt her to go into any more fashion shops. There wasn't time, in any case. They had to head for the bus stop.

Sitting on the bus, Gina started asking Annie about the Dance Club, which she'd heard about at school.

'Why?' asked Annie. 'Are you interested in coming along?'

'Yes,' Gina replied. 'I like dancing very much.'

'Do you go to lessons?' Annie asked, surprised.

'Ballet, jazz and acrobatic,' said Gina. 'I am very good.'

Annie was intrigued. 'Then you must come to our club!' she said. 'I'll remind you on Tuesday.'

Back at school on Monday, Annie and her friends got together, to compare notes. Again, Annie noticed Clemmie's absence from the group.

'How are you getting on with your visitors?' Annie asked, after she had described Gina and her uncle.

'Fine,' said Cherry. 'Anita's quite funny. She's always telling me jokes. I'm sure *I* couldn't tell anyone a joke in *Spanish!*'

'No,' sighed Annie. 'It makes us look a bit useless. Their English is so good! What about you, Pip?'

'OK, really,' Pip replied, after some hesitation. 'Manolita's no trouble at all.'

'That's the tall girl with short hair, isn't it?' asked Cherry.

'That's right,' said Pip. 'Manny adores being at the castle. She's really fit and loves swimming and riding.'

'So what about Emilia?' asked Annie. 'She's quite a quiet girl, isn't she?'

'Yes, that's the problem really,' said Pip. 'She doesn't want to join in anything. And she's scared to death of the teacher who's staying with us. She never says a *word* when she's around.'

'And what's the Señora like?' asked Annie.

Pip pulled a face. 'I'll be glad to see the back of her,' she said. 'And she's *horrible* to Emilia!'

'That's a shame,' said Cherry. 'No wonder the poor girl's frightened to say a word.'

'Like me with Mrs Ellis,' said Annie.

'You do exaggerate,' said Cherry.

'The boys are getting on fine with their students,' said Pip. 'I was talking to Sam earlier.'

'Aren't they going to move Antonia to a girl's house?' asked Cherry.

Annie felt her ears burning, as they spoke about Robbie, but didn't trust herself to say anything.

'No, she says she likes it at Robbie's,' said Pip.

'I bet she does!' cried Cherry, grinning. Then she saw Annie's face. 'Oh sorry, Annie!'

'Oh it's all right, Cherry,' Annie said quickly. 'I'm not a bit bothered about him.'

The other two exchanged looks. As luck would have it, who should walk past the group just then but Robbie and Antonia, deep in conversation.

'Oh!' cried Annie. 'These Spanish students make me sick – they speak our language far too well!'

At the Dance Club meeting the next day, Annie felt quite pleased with herself. She had introduced Gina to the club and she felt this was a friendly gesture on her part. She was still patting herself on the back when Robbie and Sam walked in, with Antonia.

'Hi,' said Sam, approaching the girls. 'We've brought Toni along. Apparently she does quite a bit of dancing back in Spain.'

Annie tried to look cool, but felt far from it. Fortunately, Cherry was taking the session today – a jazz ballet class, so she could take a back seat.

It gave her a chance to watch Gina and Toni more closely than she would have been able to.

She had to admit that they were both very able dancers – supple and strong rhythmically. Gina was one of the loosest dancers she had ever seen. When she kicked her legs at the side, they shot up to her ears, and her spine was like elastic.

She didn't mind that Toni was a good dancer. But she did mind that Toni and Robbie kept giggling together!

The class was interrupted when Mr Reynolds walked into the gym. Clemmie switched off the tape immediately, but he told her to put it back on.

'Finish what you were doing,' he said. 'What I've come to say can wait.'

A rather flustered Cherry finished the number before the headteacher would say any more.

'I've had an invitation,' he began, 'from the mayor of Shrewsbury. There is to be a big May Day celebration at Shrewsbury Castle, and he would like Bishop's to provide some outdoor entertainment. The concert band are going to give a recital, and the gym team a demonstration. But the mayor particularly asked for your Dance Club.'

Mr Reynolds smiled. Annie could hardly believe her eyes. *We must have done something right for once,* she thought. All the other members of the club looked really pleased.

'The mayor saw your version of "The Little Match Girl" at a dance festival in the New Year, and he is requesting that you do a repeat performance.'

'That would be lovely,' said Annie, on behalf of them all.

'And he also asked if you could add one other short dance item to the programme. Would that be feasible?'

'Aye,' said Annie, looking round. 'It'll be good to have something new to work on, won't it?'

Everyone nodded vigorously.

'That's settled then,' said Mr Reynolds. 'I'll write to the mayor, accepting his invitation on your behalf.'

'Well, perhaps we ought to do it ourselves, Mr Reynolds,' said Annie. 'It would seem more polite.'

Mr Reynolds looked surprised and slightly put

out. 'Yes, well, if you want to, I suppose … Come and see my secretary for some school notepaper later on.'

'That was a bit cheeky, wasn't it?' said Cherry, after the head teacher had gone.

'We don't need him to write on our behalf,' said Annie indignantly.

'It would have saved us a job,' said Cherry.

'I quite like the idea of writing to the mayor,' said Annie. 'It sounds important.'

Cherry laughed at her. 'You're daft, Annie Macdonald!'

The club members felt very excited about their first 'engagement'.

'It's almost like being professional,' said Annie dreamily, the next day.

'I suppose you're already cooking up something new for us to do?' said Pip.

'How did you guess?' asked Annie. "I've had a few ideas, but I'm not talking about them just yet, not until I firm them up a bit.'

'Won't it be exciting dancing in the castle grounds!' said Cherry.

'I hope it won't be like dancing at garden fêtes,' groaned Pip. 'D'you remember, Cherry, how awful it used to be when we were still at Miss Vane's and we had to do those really silly dances at fêtes.'

'Oh yes,' said Cherry. ' 'When the red, red robin comes bob-bob-bobbin' along …' D'you remember that one?'

Feeling a little left out of their reminiscences, Annie brought the conversation back round to May Day.

'The Spanish kids will still be here, won't they?' she asked.

'Just,' agreed Pip.

'We'd better try and include Gina and Antonia in the new dance,' said Annie. 'There isn't time to teach them "The Little Match Girl" as well.'

'Are you sure we've got time to learn a new piece?' asked Cherry. 'We've only got three and a half weeks!'

'Of course we have,' said Annie airily. 'We'll just have to have some extra evening rehearsals at the Vicarage, that's all.'

· 4 ·

Fireworks

The very first thing Annie did when she got home from dancing classes that evening was to sit down and write a letter to the mayor. She found it a little harder than she had expected and was glad the school secretary had provided her with several sheets of school notepaper. Most of these ended up in the wastepaper bin.

At last she was satisfied with her reply. She sealed it in an envelope, addressed it and took it downstairs with her.

Her mother was just serving supper.

'It's your favourite,' she said to Annie in the kitchen. 'Vegetable lasagne. Take these plates through for me, would you? Oh, and call Gina's uncle, please!'

Annie pulled a face, which her mum pretended not to notice. She took the plates to the dining-room. Gina and Louisa were already sitting at the table.

'You're keen,' Annie remarked.

'Starving, you mean,' said Louisa. Gina laughed.

'I could eat a cow!' she said.

'You mean a horse,' Annie corrected, before walking to the foot of the stairs to call Señor Bernabo.

Gina was still laughing when Annie got back – a full-blooded, throw-your-head-back guffaw, which Annie always found extremely irritating.

'Gina loves Mum's cooking,' Louisa said. 'She says they have fish nearly every day at their house.'

'That's because it's a port,' said Annie.

'What is?' asked Louisa.

'Torrievieja, where Gina comes from,' said Annie.

'That's right,' said Gina. 'Lots of fish. Tuna, sardines, shark, squid …'

'Ugh, I've heard enough,' said Louisa. 'I'm glad I'm not going to stay there,' she whispered to Annie. Annie kicked her sister under the table but Gina didn't hear Louisa's comment, as she was laughing too loudly.

Annie's parents came in with the meal but the children weren't allowed to start helping themselves, as Señor Bernabo had not yet come to the table.

Louisa looked longingly at the crispy cheese

topping on her lasagne and Annie's tummy started rumbling noisily.

'Where is he?' she muttered.

Her father shot her a warning glance from across the table, but Gina seemed quite unconcerned.

When at last Gina's uncle appeared, he sat down with only a mumbled, 'Buenos tardes.'

At bedtime, Annie tackled the subject of Señor Bernabo with Gina. She was curious to know how Gina felt about his surly behaviour, but had to be careful what she said.

'Gina,' she began, 'does your uncle live with you at your home?'

'Oh no!' cried Gina, looking amazed. 'My uncle lives in Barcelona!'

'But you see a lot of him?' Annie asked.

'No, no,' Gina replied. 'We see him one time a year, sometimes two.'

Annie didn't feel she was getting very far.

'Is he your – er – favourite uncle?' she asked.

Gina laughed uproariously. 'You think I am stupid?' she cried.

Annie looked at her. It was her turn to be amazed.

'Then why … how?' she didn't quite know how to put it tactfully.

'Why has he come to England with me?' Gina spoke for her.

Annie nodded dumbly.

'My father is his younger brother and a bit afraid of him, I think. My uncle asked him if he could accompany me on the trip and my dad said yes.'

'But why would he want to come with you, if he hardly ever sees you?' Annie asked, perplexed.

'For his researches,' Gina replied. 'He wanted to see the old houses and churches in England.'

'Is he a professor or something?' Annie asked.

'Oh no,' said Gina, laughing once more. 'He is a business man. The research is his hobby only.'

'I see,' said Annie, still feeling it didn't all quite add up. However, she felt relieved that her own impressions of Señor Bernabo weren't miles apart from Gina's.

The next morning, the whole family – plus guests – were up early, as Gina was going on an outing to the Ironbridge Gorge Museums, along with the other Spanish visitors.

At breakfast, Gina and her uncle spoke briefly in Spanish, the first such conversation that Annie had witnessed. After Señor Bernabo had left the table, Gina must have noticed Annie's curiosity, as she said—

'I asked Uncle Carlos why don't you come with us? But he said he wants to visit a round church in Shrewsbury.'

'That'll be St Chad's,' said Annie.

'I wish I was going on a trip today,' moaned Louisa. 'We've got all these SATS tests to do at school.'

'Never mind,' said Annie. 'Just do your best. You'll be fine!'

Annie's face suddenly changed colour. 'Oh no! I'd completely forgotten! We've got a biology test this morning!'

She scrambled up to find her biology book. Her nose was still in it, when Gina came to hurry her up.

'We must not be late,' said Gina. 'I shall miss the coach.'

Annie quickly packed her bag and put on her coat. She grabbed the letter to the mayor as an afterthought as she rushed out of the house.

'I won't have time to post it on the way,' she complained to Gina. 'You have to make a detour to get to the post-box.'

'Give it to me,' said Gina. 'I will post it for you in Ironbridge.'

'Thanks,' said Annie, handing over the letter. 'I hope you and Toni will join in our display at Shrewsbury Castle.'

'I would like that very much,' said Gina.

Annie's class at school seemed much smaller and quieter without the Spanish students. At break-time, she was standing with Pip and Cherry, when Clemmie walked past.

'Hi, Clemmie!' Annie called out, hoping she would join them, but she merely returned Annie's greeting and walked on.

'Who's Clemmie hanging round with these days?' Annie asked her friends.

Cherry shrugged. 'Haven't really seen her with anyone,' she said.

'Nor me,' said Pip. 'And she hasn't been busy looking after a Spanish student, because she didn't have one.'

35

'What!' Annie exclaimed. 'I never noticed, honestly. I thought she had one!'

'No, she definitely didn't,' said Pip.

'Oh maybe that's it, then,' cried Annie. 'Why she's being so quiet. Perhaps she feels left out, as we've all had Spanish girls and she hasn't.'

'Could be,' said Cherry. 'Why don't you ask her?'

The next chance Annie got, she confronted Clemmie. 'You mustn't feel out of it,' she said bluntly. 'Just because we've got Spanish guests and you haven't. We still want to talk to you, you know!'

Clemmie smiled, but her eyes didn't light up like they often did. 'You shouldn't worry so much about me, Annie,' she chided. 'I'm OK. Just feeling a bit quiet, that's all.'

'Well promise me you won't keep going off by yourself any more,' said Annie.

'Right,' said Clemmie. 'I thought you'd be a bit busy with Gina and everything.'

'Well a bit,' Annie admitted, 'but not all the time.'

Clemmie was already looking a lot happier, when the two of them met up with Pip and Cherry.

'Why didn't you have a Spanish girl to stay?' Annie asked her.

'Mum didn't want me to,' Clemmie said, in a quiet voice, and looking very uncomfortable.

Trust me to put my foot in it, Annie thought.

'Emilia's still not very happy with us,' said Pip, coming to the rescue.

'Is she still as shy?' asked Annie.

'Yes, terribly shy,' said Pip, 'but I get the feeling

she's ten times worse being with Señora Carrasco.'

'I think that's probably true,' Cherry agreed, 'because Emilia's not as bad at school, is she?'

'Or perhaps she's very homesick,' suggested Annie.

'I think she is,' said Pip. 'I can hear her crying herself to sleep every night in the next room.'

'Oh, poor girl!' cried Clemmie, looking really upset. 'I wish we could help her.'

'I do my best at home,' sighed Pip, 'but she won't talk to me. And Manny is so active and busy, she doesn't seem to notice Emilia isn't enjoying herself as much as she is.'

'We'll have to do all we can at school at any rate,' said Cherry. 'I hope none of us is homesick when we go to Spain.'

The next day was Dance Club. Annie had spent a few hours the previous evening working out ideas for a new dance. The main idea had come to her when Gina had been demonstrating some of her acrobatic skills to Louisa, earlier on.

Annie explained her suggestion to the club at lunch-time.

'The theme is "fireworks",' she said, 'so – lots of lively jumping steps, a jazzy piece of music, dazzling costumes. And also, I thought we could explore the shapes that fireworks make, you know, Catherine wheels, cascades, that sort of thing.'

Everyone seemed excited by her idea.

'Sounds great,' said Sam, 'and I think I've got just the piece of music for it.'

'Great!' cried Annie. 'Can you bring it to school tomorrow, please? Then I can get down to some serious choreography.'

'So it will be in modern style?' asked Robbie.

'Yes, that's right,' said Annie, pleased he was asking her something.

'Good,' Robbie answered, 'because Toni is really good at modern dance.'

Annie's smile faded. 'I hope Toni and Gina will enjoy taking part,' she managed to say, making a supreme effort to control her jealousy.

'What about the costumes?' asked Susie. 'They'll be really important in a piece like this.'

'Let me introduce our costume designer,' said Annie, gesturing towards Clementine. 'Of course, she'll need help with the making. We'll have to rope in as many mums as possible.'

Annie hoped Clemmie might say a few words to the club, but she looked impossibly tongue-tied.

'To help give me some ideas,' Annie continued, 'I'd like you to improvise on the fireworks theme for this session.'

She gave Clemmie a tape of 'Night on a Bare Mountain' to put on the cassette player. The club members were soon concentrating on the music and interpreting it, each in his or her own way.

Annie was impressed again by Gina's suppleness. She tried not to look at Toni too much, as Robbie was never far from her side.

By the following evening, Annie had in her hands a jazz tape from Sam and a design sketch from Clemmie.

She and Gina considered the sketch together at Annie's house.

'It is very pretty,' said Gina.

'I like it too,' said Annie.

Clemmie's drawing was based on a simple unitard. She had drawn a fountain-like sequin design on the front, and brilliant zig-zags of colour on the sleeves and legs. To complete the picture, she had added a diamanté-studded plume to the figure's head.

'I don't know if we'll afford it though,' said Annie. 'These all-in-one unitards are quite expensive to start with.'

Annie listened to Sam's tape next and saw immediately why he'd suggested it for the dance. There were little rhythmical explosions of sound and exciting percussion parts.

'This will be perfect,' said Annie, 'and you all gave me some great ideas at the club today.'

Annie needed time to think, and fortunately Gina left her to go downstairs with a book. By bedtime, she had the central part of the dance worked out. Her imagination had been fired by Gina's acrobatics, and, as she worked, she had kept seeing Gina as the main character in the piece.

Cherry and Pip had no objections to Gina being the lead when Annie made the proposal to them the following day.

'Let's ask her then,' said Cherry.

The friends went and found the group of

Spanish girls in the yard. Annie noticed that Emilia was standing a little away from the main group, looking miserable. She was easily the smallest of all the Spanish girls who were on average smaller than their English counterparts – with the exception of Manny who was even taller than Cherry. Emilia didn't have the usual Spanish colouring – she had mousy brown hair and light green eyes. Annie made a point of chatting to her, while Cherry told Gina they wanted a word with her.

When they got Gina on her own, Annie explained what they wanted her to do. 'We'd like you to dance the main role in our fireworks number,' Annie explained. 'Would you like to do it?'

Gina grinned. 'I like to do it, yes please. I think you will find I am good. I take the main role – yes – in many shows in Spain.'

'That's settled then,' said Annie quickly.

Later, she confided in Cherry that she still found Gina terribly irritating. 'I mean, she had no modesty at all when we told her she'd got the main part!'

'It's just the Spanish temperament!' said Cherry. 'Flamenco, bull-fighting – it's all a bit larger than life.'

'Mmm,' said Annie, not feeling entirely convinced. 'I hope we've done the right thing!'

The Dance Club plunged straight into rehearsals for the new dance. Everyone agreed that Annie had done a good job on the choreography, although some, particularly the ducklings, found it quite difficult and very strenuous.

Gina was brilliant in the main part, and Annie's anxieties were quickly allayed. The only problem which remained was the costumes.

'I need to get started,' said Clemmie. 'We haven't much time.'

'It's money that's the problem.' Annie sighed.

'Why don't I ask Mrs Race if she's got any suggestions?' asked Cherry.

The PE teacher had always been very supportive to the Dance Club in the past, and Annie knew that Cherry was her 'star pupil'.

'Worth a try,' Annie remarked.

When Cherry reported back later, her eyes were sparkling. 'Guess what!' she exclaimed. 'The organizers of the May Day event have given a sum of money to cover the school's expenses. And we're to have part of it for costumes!'

'Fantastic!' cried Annie. She was glad that Clemmie was with them at that moment, so that she was one of the first to hear the good news. 'You'll be able to start the costumes now!'

'Where shall we buy the unitards?' asked Clemmie. 'I can't do anything till I've got them.'

'We'll have to go to Worcester, to that brilliant Dancewear Shop, I think,' Annie answered. 'Just as soon as we've got the money.'

'Mrs Race said we'd have it tomorrow,' said Cherry.

'So we could go on Saturday. I'll persuade my

41

mum to take us.'

'I love going back to that shop,' cried Annie. 'I'll never forget being fitted there for my first pair of pointe shoes.'

'You'll love it, Clemmie,' said Cherry. 'Especially the gorgeous tutus they have on display.'

The other members of the class started coming back into the classroom just then. It was a terrific squash when all the Spanish students came in as well. Gina smiled at Annie as she sat down in an adjacent desk. Annie noticed she had come in with Maria and Zoë, but put it down to coincidence. It prompted her to remember, however, what a lot of trouble Maria used to make when she was a member of the Dance Club. Thank goodness the friends had been able to persuade her to leave of her own accord, as Mr Reynolds would never have allowed them to get rid of her otherwise.

Just as Mrs Clanger was taking the afternoon register, Mr Reynolds walked in.

'Excuse me, Mrs Clanger,' the headteacher began, 'but I would like a quick word with Annie Macdonald.'

Annie's heart began to thump as she stood up and moved over to the teacher's desk.

'Now, young lady, I think you told me you were writing the letter of acceptance to the mayor on your club's behalf.'

'Yes sir,' said Annie, feeling slightly puzzled.

'Well, I've just had a phone call. No such letter has arrived and they're wondering if the Dance

42

Club doesn't want to take part, after all.'

'Oh no!' said Annie. 'I mean, yes we *do* want to take part and I *did* write a letter to the mayor. I remember p ...' She couldn't finish her sentence, as she suddenly recollected handing the envelope to Gina.

She glanced round at the Spanish girl, but she was not looking in the slightest bit concerned.

'I note your hesitation,' said Mr Reynolds. 'I don't know how you could have forgotten to post such an important letter! But I'll get the secretary to write one this afternoon. Then there'll be absolutely *no* doubt it will get to the mayor in time.'

Annie was still hoping Gina might leap to her feet, to admit responsibility, but Mr Reynolds was half-way out of the door and Gina was still sitting in her seat, with her mouth firmly shut.

Feeling very small, with everyone's gaze upon her, Annie sank back into her own chair. *If only I could be somewhere else right now*, she thought.

When she had recovered sufficiently, she cast a quick glance over in Robbie's direction. What she saw made her feel even worse. He and Toni were whispering and giggling together, and Toni was looking straight at Annie!

5

The Secretive Señor

Annie was seething all the way home on the bus.
Gina sat beside her, as usual, but Annie hardly
spoke a word the whole journey. Even Gina – not
the most sensitive of people – realized there was
something wrong, but she put off tackling Annie
until they got home.

'You are upset – no?' Gina began, after she had
followed Annie to her room.

Annie felt ready to explode, but reminded
herself just in time that Gina was a guest in her
home, and that her parents might not take too
kindly to such an outburst.

She swallowed hard.

'I am upset, yes,' she replied. 'I got into trouble

with the headteacher because you forgot to post my letter!'

'I am sorry,' said Gina, with her most winning smile. She shrugged her shoulders and brought up her hands expressively.

'I must have dropped it. But your Mr Reynolds – he is writing you another one.'

She turned away as though that's all there was to be said, and started to unpack her school bag.

Annie was still smouldering, but felt it would be a waste of time to take it any further. She didn't respond much to Gina's chatter, however, with the result that the Spanish girl soon left her alone in the bedroom.

This at least helped Annie to recover her spirits. She wrote up her diary, pouring out her feelings of injustice on to the page, and then decided to find a good book to read. Unusually, no homework had been set and it was a night free from dancing lessons.

She hunted through her bookcase but could find nothing she hadn't read before. She considered reading *Ballet Shoes* for the fifth time, but decided against it. Then she remembered the bookcase in the spare bedroom. There might be something new to her there.

Knowing that Gina's uncle was still out, on a visit to Hodnet Hall, Annie crept into the spare room and knelt down by the bookcase. She pulled out a book. It was called *Midnight Blue*. She opened it and read the first page. It sounded interesting. She read on.

Next moment, there was a torrent of Spanish cascading around her ears. Looking up, Annie saw the angry face of Señor Bernabo, bending over her.

She shot to her feet, her heart pounding.

'Sorry,' she stammered. 'I mean I just wanted to get a book, uno …' She held up the novel to show him what she meant.

He still looked very cross – his thin face had grown extremely red, and he was still spouting Spanish phrases that Annie hadn't a hope of understanding.

Annie backed out of the room, clutching the book to her chest. Señor Bernabo followed her on to the landing, but then seemed to think better of it, and went back into his room.

'Phew!' whispered Annie, as she reached the safety of her bedroom. She was beginning to feel really fed up with her Spanish visitors.

Having received the money for the costumes, Annie went ahead with her planned trip to Worcester.

There was an argument at home on the Friday, when Annie's mum realized there wouldn't be room for Gina in the car.

'But we *must* bring Gina with us!' she exclaimed, in the privacy of the kitchen.

'We can't, Mum,' Annie wailed. 'I've promised Cherry and Pip and Clemmie. It wouldn't be fair to leave anyone out now!'

'But we have a responsibility to look after Gina,' said Mrs Macdonald.

Gina was still far from being Annie's favourite person. 'Well, we *can't* bring her. There just won't be room.'

Mrs Macdonald sighed heavily. 'No, I'm sorry. You'll just have to put off one of your friends.'

Annie knew the look on her mother's face. It meant she was not to be argued with further.

Reluctantly, she went to the telephone. The problem was *who* should she choose to put off. Clemmie was the obvious choice, but she didn't think she had the heart to disappoint her. But there again, whoever she chose out of Pip or Cherry would be jealous of the other. It was a dilemma.

She decided to put off her decision until she'd come back from her ballet lesson with Miss Rodelle – unless she told Cherry at the studio.

It was a joy to be at the studio – everything was properly fitted now – barres, mirrors, good heating. Even the waiting and changing rooms were fully equipped and newly redecorated.

Cherry noticed that Annie was rather quiet, and asked her if anything was wrong. In the end, Annie decided to confide in her friend.

'I just don't know what to do!' Annie cried.

'Well, I've just thought of the perfect solution,' said Cherry. 'I don't think my dad's busy tomorrow. He loves going to Worcester cathedral. I'm sure he'd drive me up there!'

Annie beamed at her. 'Oh Cherry,' she said, 'I'm so glad I told you!'

After a very enjoyable ballet lesson, Annie went home and told her mother the good news.

The next morning, a small convoy of two cars set off from the Vicarage, which had been chosen as a central meeting point. Pip travelled with Cherry and the vicar, while Annie, Clemmie, Louisa and Gina went with Annie's mum.

Mrs Macdonald and Louisa went off shopping once they had parked, and Mr Stevens headed for Cathedral Close, leaving the girls to make their way to the Dancewear Shop on their own.

Annie still hadn't quite forgiven Gina. Once in the shop, Gina's irrepressible exuberance at the sight of so many lovely costumes brought a smile to many faces. To Annie's surprise, she found that Gina and Clemmie were getting on rather well. As Pip and Cherry were mooching round together, it was Annie who ended up feeling a little on her own.

But quite soon, Clemmie called her over to help her decide which unitard would be best for the costumes.

In the end, the girls decided to buy unitards in several different bright shades – green, gold, red and blue – the most popular firework colours.

'Perhaps we ought only to get *one* gold costume, for Gina,' Clemmie suggested. 'She ought to stand out from the rest.'

When Annie agreed readily, Gina squealed and

clapped her hands. Several customers turned to stare, surprised that such a smartly dressed young lady should be behaving in this childish manner. Annie found her behaviour in public quite embarrassing.

However, by the time they got back to Shrewsbury, Annie was feeling a lot more relaxed with Gina.

She had invited Clemmie to stay for tea. The three girls went up to Annie's room before the meal, and sat on the bed playing cards. When Louisa called Gina downstairs to show her some more acrobatics, Annie asked Clemmie if she were feeling happier now at school.

'Oh yes,' said Clemmie, looking at her feet, 'but I *do* wish I'd had a Spanish student.'

'You can have Gina and her uncle with pleasure!' whispered Annie.

Clemmie laughed. 'Gina's really nice, but I don't know about her uncle. It would just have been fun having someone staying with me. It's so quiet at our house – not a bit like yours.'

As Clemmie spoke, peals of laughter could be heard from downstairs.

'Well, why wouldn't your mum let you?' asked Annie.

Clemmie looked uncomfortable, and then shrugged. 'Perhaps she thought it would be too much of a strain on me.'

Their conversation was interrupted when Louisa called them both down for tea.

49

A few days later, the subject of the Spanish students cropped up again. Annie and her friends were standing talking in the gym after a Dance Club rehearsal.

'It's really nice having Gina and Toni included in our dances,' Cherry said. 'They add quite a "zip" don't you think?'

'The ones that join in are so much easier than the ones who don't,' said Pip.

'D'you mean Emilia?' Annie asked.

'Got it in one,' Pip answered. 'I feel very sorry for her, but it's boring having to look after her.'

As they crossed the yard, back to the form room, they approached Manny and Emilia who were talking to one another. Annie noticed Señora Carrasco walk over to them and begin shouting and waving her arms around.

'Goodness!' cried Annie. 'Whatever is she going on about?'

'It won't be anything important,' said Pip. 'She just likes the sound of her own voice.'

As they passed the small group of Spaniards, Annie saw that Emilia was crying.

'She's a bit of a bully, that woman, isn't she?'

'It must be awful for Emilia to be staying at the same house as Señora Carrasco,' said Clemmie thoughtfully. She paused and then added, 'I think I'll ask my mother if she'll let me have her to stay at our house.'

'That would be great!' cried Pip. 'Manny and I could go off riding and things much more then. And it would certainly make Emilia a lot happier!'

'Then I'll ask,' Clemmie promised.

Annie could tell by the triumphant look on Clemmie's face the next morning that she had succeeded in her request. Pip wasted no time in telling Emilia, and introduced her properly to Clemmie.

'You'd have your own room,' said Clemmie, 'but I'm afraid ours is a *much* smaller house than Pip's.'

'*Everyone*'s house is much smaller than Pip's,' laughed Annie.

'I do not mind,' said Emilia, who was looking happier than the friends had seen her all visit. 'I like to come to your home, please!'

The move was arranged quickly, and everyone was happier for it, except perhaps for Señora Carrasco, who had lost her favourite victim.

Rehearsals for May Day were well under way by now, as were the costumes, under Clemmie's supervision. Mrs Macdonald was to make Annie's and the twins', but Clemmie had reserved Gina's for herself.

'It's going to be a bit special,' she told the others, whenever they enquired about it.

The only thing left to fix was the name of the modern 'fireworks' piece. They were all talking about it one day at Dance Club, and numerous suggestions were made – 'Rockets', 'Flashes and

Bangs' and 'Jumping Jacks' among them. But the suggestion Annie liked best was made by Robbie – 'Squib!'

'I think that's a great name,' she said enthusiastically. 'It's short and strong – it's just right!'

'Let's vote then, shall we?' said Cherry. The majority of the club members voted for Robbie's suggestion, so 'Squib' was adopted as the dance's name.

'Something that worries me,' said Annie, at the next meeting, 'is that we have only rehearsed this – and "The Little Match Girl" – indoors. It's going to feel very different outside.'

'In our next evening rehearsal at my house,' said Cherry, 'we could use the front lawn.'

'Or how about coming to Totley!' suggested Pip. 'That would really give us the feel of dancing in front of a castle!'

'Brilliant!' cried Annie. 'Why didn't I think of that!'

'Why don't we try and get the costumes ready for it, and I could take some great photos?' Sam added.

'Then we could put some of the best one in the local newspaper, to advertise the May Day,' said Annie. 'Great!'

'And if it's going to be a dress rehearsal,' said Pip, 'why don't we charge a small entrance fee? I know a lot of the local people would like to come and see us, and we could invite our mums and dads too!'

'We could raise some money for charity,' Cherry suggested.

A date was fixed for a week before May Day and pressure was put on all the volunteer dressmakers to finish the costumes by then. The Dance Club had to work very hard too, to learn and perfect their new dance in the short time that was left.

In record time, all the costumes were finished and brought to school for everyone to try on and admire. Clemmie wouldn't let anyone see Gina's costume until the next Dance Club meeting. She brought it in under an old sheet, and unveiled it in front of the assembled club members.

An *ah!* of admiration ran around the group in the gym. The costume was truly dazzling. Even the zig-zags had been marked out in row upon row of sequins.

'It's terrific!' cried Annie. Gina looked pleased, obviously, but not as excited as other people might have been, Annie thought. She rather had the air of 'I've seen it and done it all before'. But Annie had no doubt that Gina would look simply stunning in the costume. She thanked her lucky stars that she hadn't put *Toni* in the main role!

Sam had come, armed with his camera and the session was almost entirely taken up with photographing the dancers in their costumes, in grouped tableaux arranged by Annie and Cherry.

'We might as well get a photo in the paper in time to advertise Totley as well,' Sam explained.

Clemmie had received so many congratulations from the dancers on her successful design that Annie was surprised to see her still looking quite unhappy a few days later.

'Everything OK? with Emilia?' she asked her friend.

'Emilia?' Clemmie repeated, almost vacantly. 'Oh, yes, everything's fine. She seems much happier away from the terrible Señora.'

'And what about you?' asked Annie. 'Is everything fine with you?'

'Yes, of course,' said Clemmie, but Annie could tell she was lying. It was exasperating. She really had thought with the success of the costumes, and having a Spanish girl at home like the rest of the gang, Clemmie would have been walking on air!

6

A Big Splash

Annie began to see much less of Clemmie from then on, as she became even busier with rehearsals for their display. Clemmie was more absorbed herself with taking care of Emilia, in any case, so Annie didn't feel too guilty.

With one less worry on her mind, Annie threw herself into preparations for their performance at Totley Castle. The club decided to lay on refreshments afterwards, to be served on the lawn, so a list was circulated around their parents asking for contributions of food and drink. Cherry's dad had a good computer and printer at home, so she offered to produce the tickets and programmes.

Then, of course, there was much discussion over

which charity would benefit from their performance. A popular suggestion was 'Children in Need' but an equal number of members wanted to support the Oxfam refugee appeal. No one could decide.

Annie, beginning to feel exasperated that precious rehearsal time was slipping away, took a stand.

'As we're never going to reach an agreement,' she said, 'I propose that Pip should make the final decision, as it's her family home that we're throwing open to the public.'

When there was general assent to this proposal, Pip chose the refugee appeal.

The next bit of excitement was when one of Sam's photos made a big splash in the *Shropshire Star*, thanks to Annie's dad who had had a word in the sub-editor's ear. Every member of the club came to school with a copy of the newspaper the morning following the publication of the photograph.

'It's terrific!' said Annie to Sam. 'It just looks like a professional job.'

'I didn't think they'd print it in colour,' said Sam looking rather proud. It looks pretty good doesn't it?'

'Magnificent!' exclaimed Gina. She looked particularly stunning in the photo and was bang in the middle of it.

'Dad's done a good write-up too,' said Annie. 'It'll give us marvellous publicity for both performances, won't it?'

'I hope we live up to it!' said Pip, looking a little anxious.

'All we've got to do is work hard now, and go for it!' cried Annie.

That evening, Gina seemed very pleased with herself. She made a point of showing Louisa and Mrs Macdonald the photo in the paper, even though they'd seen it before.

'It's the best picture of me I ever see,' she said proudly.

'You look great!' said Louisa enthusiastically. 'Tons better than Annie.'

Annie had to agree. It was not a very flattering photo of her – she had been in the middle of a blink when Sam took it.

Gina was so delighted that she gave away several items of make-up to the eager Louisa. At bedtime, she gazed at herself in the wardrobe mirror, striking different model-like poses.

'Do you think I am beautiful?' she asked.

Annie was already in bed. She grunted and pulled the duvet over her head.

'Hurry up and switch the light off,' she complained.

As the rehearsals sped by, Annie began to realize with a mounting feeling of panic, that she had been over-ambitious with her choreography of 'Squib'.

Something which irritated her, and interfered with her concentration, was Maria's new habit of popping into the gym at odd times to watch the rehearsals. She had become very friendly with

Gina, and Annie felt most unwilling to tell the Spanish girl the full story of how Maria had been forced to leave Dance Club. It therefore became difficult to object to Maria's presence as an observer, when Gina was so obviously delighted by it. She was a born performer, and even an audience of one was better than none.

But Maria being there, even for part of the time, was a thorn in Annie's side. The three friends tried to drop a few hints, without being too obvious in front of Gina, but Maria was thick-skinned, as usual.

Feeling more and more alarmed by the lack of progress of 'Squib' in particular, Annie called a 'special meeting' of the 'big three', as they sometimes called themselves, at Cherry's house.

Cherry's Spanish visitor, Anita, wasn't the nosy type, and the girls knew she wouldn't want to intrude on their meeting. It would have been difficult to be private at Annie's, with Gina bounding around.

When they had settled into Cherry's bedroom, Annie began:

' "Squib" isn't going to be ready, is it?' she said glumly. 'At least not for Totley.'

'It's got to be ready!' cried Cherry. 'I've included it on the programmes. They're all printed now!'

'And the photo in the *Star* was of us in our "Squib" costumes,' Pip pointed out. 'People will be disappointed if they come to the castle and don't see any sign of the dance that was advertised.'

58

'I know, I know,' Annie sighed, 'but we can't let it be shown to the public until it's polished.'

'We've still got a few days,' said Cherry. 'And we've got two extra rehearsals here. I'm sure we'll be fine. It's always like this just before a show.'

Annie still looked worried. 'If only Maria hadn't been plaguing us again!' she said.

'Don't let her bother you,' said Cherry. 'She can't do any more harm to us. She can only observe. Just ignore her!'

'I can't,' said Annie. 'She makes me nervous.'

'Then we shall have to be firm with her,' said Cherry. 'I hadn't realized it was upsetting you so much. Next time she turns up, I'll ask her how Fred is, very pointedly.'

Annie's face brightened. 'Fred' was their pet name for Maria's brother's plastic skeleton, which she had 'borrowed' to play a stupid trick on Annie and her friends. They had promised not to reveal what Maria had done, provided she left the Dance Club of her own accord, and made no more trouble.

'That should do the trick,' said Pip, laughing. 'I shouldn't think we'll see Maria for dust!'

'I'm not so sure,' said Annie. 'She thinks she's got a foothold again, through her friendship with Gina.'

'Trust those two to get together,' tutted Cherry.

'Mmm,' Annie agreed. 'Not the best thing that could have happened. Of course, Maria is very good at sucking up to people when she thinks she can get something out of it. And Gina's just the sort that would fall for it in a big way.'

'The star of stage and screen!' laughed Pip.

'Something like that,' said Annie. 'Anyway, if you would tackle Maria, Cherry, I'll announce to the club that we'll only be performing "The Little Match Girl" at Totley.'

'What!' Cherry exclaimed. 'But we can't cancel "Squib"!'

'No, we can't, Annie,' said Pip. 'Apart from anything else, Gina would be furious!'

Annie's mouth set in a stubborn line. 'I'm not letting the club put something on which might damage its reputation.'

'But it's only at Totley!' Pip exclaimed. 'It won't be a huge audience.'

'You never know who's going to be in our audience,' Annie pointed out. 'There could be a talent scout, who knows?'

In the end, Annie won the argument as usual. As luck would have it, Maria turned up at the beginning of the next club meeting, just as Annie was making her announcement about 'Squib'.

As Pip had predicted, Gina went wild. 'You can't do it!' she cried. 'All these rehearsals! And my costume!'

'We shall still do "Squib" on May Day,' Annie said, placatingly. 'And we'll rehearse it at Totley in the morning, to give us a chance of doing it outdoors.'

'That's a bit tough on Gina, isn't it?' said Maria,

moving in like a cobra for the kill. 'She isn't in "The Little Match Girl", is she? Which means she won't be in the Totley display at all.'

Tears of fury and disappointment were welling from Gina's eyes.

'Why don't you keep your nose out, Maria!' cried Annie.

'I hate your club!' yelled Gina. 'I leave it today! And you never see me again!'

Gina made a dramatic exit at this point, followed by a very satisfied-looking Maria.

Everyone else stood about, looking rather shocked.

'Well, at least we won't have to tell Maria not to keep coming to club meetings,' said Cherry, attempting a smile.

Annie didn't dare look at either Cherry or Pip, in case she read in their expressions the message 'I told you so!'.

'What are we going to do now?' asked Pip, when the three friends were left on their own in the gym.

Annie found it difficult to say anything at all, as she knew this catastrophe was all of her own making.

'Perhaps she'll come round,' said Cherry. 'By May Day, I mean. She's probably the sort of person who explodes, and then thinks better of it.'

'She could be,' said Pip. 'But she *did* look awfully upset. And with Maria winding her up …'

'Yes, that's true,' said Cherry. 'We all know what mischief Maria can do.'

'Couldn't someone else take Gina's part?' asked Pip, looking now at Annie.

Annie shook herself out of the cocoon she had climbed into, to protect herself from feeling too guilty. 'Nay,' she replied, shaking her head miserably. 'There's no one else who can do acrobatic dance.'

'Not even Toni?' asked Pip.

'No!' Annie cried emphatically.

Pip and Cherry exchanged glances.

'Well, could you change the part, so it's not so acrobatic?' asked Cherry.

'There just isn't time for someone to learn a new part, even if I did,' said Annie. ' "Squib" will just have to be dropped from our programme on May Day as well.'

'It's such a shame,' said Cherry. 'After all that hard work on the costumes too!'

This was something Annie hadn't yet thought about. It was like a stab in the ribs. However would she be able to break the news to Clemmie?

'Oh!' she said, her eyes brimming with tears. 'This is all my fault.'

'Perhaps if you told Gina you'd changed your mind about Totley …' Cherry suggested, putting her arm round her friend.

'I think it's too late for that,' sobbed Annie.

The next few days were very difficult. Annie felt as if all the club members were blaming her for Gina's departure. At home, Gina was refusing to say a word to her, which, as they shared a bedroom, felt very uncomfortable indeed.

But the very worst thing was telling Clemmie that they wouldn't be needing the 'Squib' costumes after all.

'You're joking!' said Clemmie.

'Nay,' said Annie. 'I'm not.'

She described the whole episode, which had led to Gina's pulling out.

'I see,' said Clemmie quietly.

Annie would have much preferred Clemmie to shout at her.

'But I'm sure we'll be able to use the costumes for our next show,' she said quickly.

'When will that be?' asked Clemmie.

'I don't know yet, but …' Annie began.

'I see,' Clemmie said again, with an air of resignation.

'We *shall* use them,' said Annie. 'They're such brilliant costumes.'

'Hmmmm,' said Clemmie.

That night, which was the third night after the row, Annie decided she must try her very best to heal the rift with Gina. It was bedtime, the only chance she had to get Gina on her own.

'Look, Gina, I'm *really* sorry,' she began.

No reply.

'Can't we talk about this?'

No reply.

'I don't want to fall out with you, I really don't.

63

What can I say to make you less angry with me? said Annie.

'Nothing,' said Gina.

That Gina was speaking to her at all was a bit of progress. Encouraged, Annie continued –

'Won't you come back to Dance Club, Gina?' she asked. 'We really need you for our May Day show.'

Gina snorted. 'I not come back to Dance Club if it is the *last* club in the world.'

'But there's no one else who can dance the lead in "Squib",' Annie pressed on. 'None of the rest of us are as acrobatic as you.'

A sort of smile appeared on Gina's face. 'You should have thought of that before,' she said.

'Oh please, Gina!' Annie begged. 'Pretend I never said anything. You can come to Totley Castle – we'll do "Squib" there in front of the public. You'll be a star!'

But not even this appeal to Gina's vanity would work.

'I told you,' Gina said icily, with a dramatic toss of her head. 'I never come back to your club. Never! Maria told me you cannot be trusted. I see she is right!'

· 7 ·

Another Big Splash

There was no alternative but to scrap 'Squib' altogether and press ahead with their rehearsals of 'The Little Match Girl'. Annie still felt very guilty and uneasy, especially where Clemmie and Gina were concerned. Robbie seemed cross with her too, as it meant of course that Toni wouldn't be dancing in either performance.

Annie made a point of inviting both Gina and Toni to come along to Totley with the club anyway, to help with ticket sales and serving refreshments. Toni accepted quite happily – she seemed an easy-going sort of girl – but Gina (as Annie had expected) refused.

The day before the Totley display, Annie's

family, plus Spanish guests, were sitting round the dinner table when Mr Macdonald said the newspaper had received some news which might interest Annie and Gina. (Annie's parents didn't yet know that Gina had left the Dance Club.)

'What is it, Dad?' asked Annie.

'There's been a break-in up at Shrewsbury Castle,' he replied. 'An attempted burglary, by the look of it. Fortunately, they failed to put one of the alarms out of action, and got frightened off before they'd taken anything.'

'What is there to steal in the castle?' asked Annie.

'Oh, a wealth of art treasures,' said her father. 'And in particular, a painting by Degas. The police think that was their main target.'

'But May Day is still going ahead?' asked Annie, suddenly feeling anxious.

'Oh yes, there'd be no reason to stop it,' said her dad, 'but I imagine they'll step up security. They probably won't allow admission to the galleries while it's going on.'

'That's a shame,' said Annie. 'I'd like to have seen the paintings.'

'You'll probably be able to, when you go up for your run-through next week,' said her mum. She turned to Gina. 'Are you looking forward to performing at two castles?' she asked her, with a smile.

Gina glowered at Annie. 'I no longer in the Dance Club,' she said in a tragic voice.

Of course, this set off a host of questions which

Annie had to answer. It ended up with her leaving three-quarters of her dinner on her plate and rushing up to her bedroom in tears. Even here, there was no privacy, as Gina followed her up soon after.

Annie buried her face in the pillow and wished as hard as she could that Gina would go away. She could hear Gina moving about the room, opening drawers, and coughing as if she were a bit embarrassed. Before much longer, she left the room, much to Annie's relief.

Annie didn't sleep at all well and felt very glad to be going out early the following day. Cherry's parents picked her up and they set off for Pip's before it was even nine o'clock. They wanted to be there in good time, to get everything ready for the refreshments.

'Have you got the tickets and programmes?' Annie asked, while they were pulling away from her house.

'Yes, let me show you,' said Cherry excitedly. 'I managed to change the programmes on the computer and print some new ones, leaving out "Squib".'

'Oh thanks, Cherry,' said Annie. 'You've done a great job.'

'Mum's been cooking too,' said Cherry. 'There's masses of cakes in the boot.'

'Brilliant!' cried Annie, cheering up a lot. The morning sped by. There was such a lot to do. And their dress rehearsal took longer than they'd anticipated. So much effort had been put into 'Squib' over the preceding weeks, that 'The Little Match Girl' had grown a little rusty.

But at last Annie was satisfied, and they broke for a late lunch. The performance was scheduled for 3.30. After she'd given the club last minute instructions, they dispersed in the grounds to eat their packed lunches. Fortunately it was a clear, fine day and plenty warm enough to be comfortable out of doors. They had planned to use the Banqueting Hall in case of wet weather.

After she had finished picnicking, with Pip and Cherry, Annie fancied a little walk on her own. She was still feeling quite stressed from the Gina episode, and thought it might clear her head a little. She struck out across the grounds, and had soon left behind the rest of her colleagues.

Reaching a high wall, with a door set in it, she let herself into a small walled garden where a variety of herbs and vegetables were growing, alongside flowering shrubs and lilac trees. She stood at the doorway, entranced. *This is just like* The Secret Garden, she thought to herself. It was surprising that Pip had never taken her to it before. But there again, Pip took so many unusual features about her home for granted, that she ought not to be surprised.

Annie became aware suddenly that she was not alone in the garden. There was some movement behind the lilac. She stood very still. Robbie and Toni were sitting on a garden seat, facing one another. They were holding hands and completely unaware of Annie's presence.

Holding her breath, she backed out through the open door. Then she ran towards the castle, as if she were being chased by a horde of angry wasps.

She arrived panting at the kitchen, where Cherry and Pip were putting the finishing touches to the refreshments.

'Is it time to get changed?' asked Pip.

'You look as though something's after you,' Cherry exclaimed.

Annie looked at her watch. 'Aye, it's time we got ready,' she said, ignoring Cherry's remark.

Distracted by the thought that Robbie and Antonia were getting *so* friendly, Annie found it a hard task to concentrate fully on her dancing. She made several slips in her part as Chief Angel, which in turn threw the other angels, who were meant to take her lead. They were silly mistakes, in quite easy passages. *You've got to get a grip!* she told herself. *You're going to ruin everything!*

By the time she reached the more difficult solo passages, and parts when only she and Susie were dancing, she had regained her concentration. Susie was dancing the Little Match Girl role beautifully, and at the end of their ballet, the small, but delighted audience, gave them a long round of applause.

'That was lovely!' one elderly lady enthused to Annie and her friends, as they were moving about among the audience, with trays of cakes and scones. 'I haven't been able to get to a theatre for years. And to see such a wonderful ballet on my own doorstep was a real treat!'

When the old lady's two friends joined her in congratulating the girls, Annie began to think perhaps it had been worth it.

Just then, a tremendous commotion began behind them.

'He's fallen in!' they heard people yelling. The girls ran to the crowd who had assembled at the edge of the lake.

A distraught young woman was sobbing despairingly, calling, 'Timmy! Timmy!' from time to time.

'Ring an ambulance!' someone shouted. 'A child's fallen in the lake!'

Pip ran off immediately to make the phone call. Annie and Cherry stared, horrified, at the water. There was absolutely no sign of the child. The water was quite calm. He must have sunk to the bottom.

'Pip said it was very deep, didn't she?' hissed Cherry, kicking off her shoes.

'What are you doing?' asked Annie, wide-eyed.

Cherry was stripping off her costume.

'I'm going in,' she said, with a determined expression.

'But you don't know where he is …' Annie began.

Cherry looked at the water once more, and Annie followed her gaze. A single bubble appeared just to their left, like a sign from heaven.

'That's it,' said Cherry, gritting her teeth. She ran a little way down the bank and dived into the icy water. Annie closed her eyes. She couldn't bear it if anything happened to her friend. But then, she told herself, of all the people at the castle, Cherry was probably the best athlete, the strongest swimmer. If anyone could save little Timmy, it was Cherry.

She opened her eyes. Cherry had surfaced, but there was no sign of the boy. Annie sent up a fervent silent prayer as Cherry duck-dived and disappeared into the depths of the lake once more.

A man ran up to the distraught lady. It was Timmy's father, who had been elsewhere in the castle grounds and had only just learned of his son's accident. As he started to take off his shoes, Cherry resurfaced. She was still empty-handed. She gasped and took several lungfuls of air before going down once more. Timmy's father plunged in at about the same moment. Seconds ticked by when there was no sign on the surface of the lake that there was anyone beneath it. There was a gasp from the crowd. Cherry had come up clutching Timmy. The little boy was as limp as a rag doll. Cherry, for all her strength as a swimmer, looked exhausted. Annie wondered frantically how far down she had had to dive to reach him.

Timmy's father broke surface a fraction of a second later, his lungs bursting. His wife was by now hysterical. He and Cherry brought Timmy to the bank between them. There was still no flicker of life in his body.

The local doctor, who fortunately had been a member of the audience, had by now come to the lakeside and was waiting to receive the casualty. He calmly reassured Timmy's parents as he systematically drained the water from their son's lungs and began resuscitation.

He continued to give him the kiss of life, until the paramedic team arrived with the ambulance. Just after this, Timmy began to breathe unaided, and the doctor said he had a reasonable pulse, considering what he'd been through. He even began to regain a little colour to his face.

Pip had wrapped Cherry in a huge blanket and offered one to Timmy's father also. When she tried to take her indoors Cherry insisted on waiting until she had seen Timmy safely tucked up on the stretcher. As the little boy was carried into the ambulance, accompanied by his mother, Cherry agreed to go in to get dry. Timmy's father said he would follow on by car. On his way to his car, he stopped and asked Annie for Cherry's name and phone number.

'She was so brave,' he said, through chattering teeth. 'We can never thank her enough.'

Annie gave him her name and number and went off to the house, to see how Cherry was getting along.

'I'm fine,' said Cherry. 'Just ravenously hungry.'

'You won't be for long,' said Pip. 'I'm going to pile your plate with cakes.'

'Is Timmy going to be all right?' Cherry asked Annie.

'Aye, I think so,' Annie replied. 'I heard one of the ambulance men say to his mother that he would be OK.' She told Cherry about the encounter with Timmy's father. 'He'll probably phone you,' she said.

The next day – Sunday – Annie popped over to Cherry's. She wanted to talk about the events at Totley once more with her friend, and had also decided to tell her what she had seen in the walled garden.

'Guess what,' Cherry said, as soon as she had let her in. 'Timmy's dad wants to give me a reward! I said I didn't want anything, just to know Timmy's going to be all right was quite enough. But he insisted!'

'When are you going to get it?' asked Annie. 'And what will it be?'

'I don't know what it will be,' said Cherry, 'but Mr Rodding has asked me to go round to his shop in Shrewsbury tomorrow afternoon to collect it!'

'Where's his shop exactly?' Annie asked.

'Down the Wyle Cop,' Cherry answered. 'Up a little alley-way. It's a picture gallery.'

'Oh, I know it,' said Annie. 'Perhaps he'll give you a picture!'

Cherry grimaced. 'A box of chocolates would be better! But we'll just have to wait and see!'

'Cherry,' said Annie. 'I didn't tell you yesterday what I saw in the grounds.'

'No, what *did* you see in the grounds?'

'Well, it was in this walled garden, just like *The Secret Garden*.'

'What was?'

'That I saw them together!' exclaimed Annie.

'Who?' asked Cherry. 'You're not making any sense.'

'Robbie and Toni of course!' cried Annie. 'Who else?'

'Not everyone goes around thinking about Robbie and Toni, and nothing else,' said Cherry.

'Nor do I!' said Annie indignantly.

'Well anyway,' said Cherry. 'What about it?'

'What about what?'

'What about you seeing them together?'

'Oh,' said Annie. 'They were sitting on this bench all private and tucked away, gazing into each other's eyes, and *holding hands*!'

Cherry giggled.

'It's not funny!' Annie said. 'He must really like her. And I'm never going to have a chance to have a date with him!'

'What d'you mean, "never"?' cried Cherry. 'She'll be gone in just over a week.'

Annie's face brightened. 'You're right,' she said. 'And he'll probably never see her again.'

'He will in October,' said Cherry.

'No he won't,' Annie contradicted her. 'Don't you remember, Robbie's not making the return visit.'

'Oh yes he is,' said Cherry. 'Sorry to disappoint you.'

'What d'you mean?' Annie demanded.

'Haven't you heard? Robbie's dad's got a new job – a really well paid one, so he can afford to go to Spain after all.'

'Oh no!' yelled Annie, leaping to her feet. 'I had no idea!'

'October's a long way away,' said Cherry wisely. 'Plenty of time for Robbie to forget all about Toni and fall under your spell again.'

Annie didn't feel at all confident that this was the way it would be, but she was grateful to Cherry for trying to make her feel better. She volunteered to go to the gallery next day with her friend to pick up the reward.

'I wonder what it will be?' said Annie, on their way there. 'Perhaps he'll give you a thousand pounds.'

'Somehow I doubt it,' said Cherry.

'You never know,' said Annie. 'He and his wife must be ever so grateful to you for saving their son's life.'

As they went down the little alley-way, Annie clutched Cherry's arm.

'Look who's coming out of the shop!' she hissed.

It was Señor Bernabo, carrying a parcel under his arm. Annie pulled Cherry back out of the alley and they stood in a shop doorway, until the Spaniard had gone past.

'I didn't want to bump into *him*,' she explained. 'He gives me the creeps!'

'It looked as if he'd bought a picture from Mr Rodding,' said Cherry, as they made their way down the alley once more.

In the shop, they had to wait a few minutes, as Mr Rodding was helping a customer. So they went round the small gallery, looking at all the lovely pictures that were for sale.

'I love this one!' Annie exclaimed, coming to rest in front of a painting of a group of ballet dancers rehearsing in an old-fashioned studio.

'You've very good taste,' said a voice behind her. It was Mr Rodding. 'Unfortunately mine is only a print. The real thing is by Degas and it's hanging in Shrewsbury Castle at the moment.'

'Isn't that the very valuable one?' Annie asked.

'That's right,' said Mr Rodding. 'It's insured for three million!'

'Wow!' said the girls in chorus.

'Now, Cherry,' said Mr Rodding. 'I want to thank you again for what you did on Saturday. Timmy's making very good progress, his doctors say. All thanks to you.'

Cherry went red, but managed to say,

'Can I go and visit him?'

'Of course,' said Mr Rodding, beaming. He opened a drawer in his desk and took out a small package.

'Here you are,' he said. 'To commemorate a very brave deed.'

'Thank you very much,' said Cherry, still very pink. 'But I really didn't think about it being dangerous!'

'I'll write down Timmy's ward number for you. He's in Shrewsbury hospital. I know he'd be very glad to meet the young lady who saved his life.'

Once they were outside, Cherry's blushes faded.

'Oh I could have *died* with embarrassment,' she said.

'Come on, then, open it!' Annie urged her.

8

A Suspicious Conversation

'Mr Rodding has been very generous to you,' said
Mrs Stevens, after Cherry had shown her the
contents of her package. She had been given a
small statuette of a dancer, modelled in bronze.

'It's so kind of the Roddings!' cried Cherry.
'They needn't have given me anything!'

'She's beautiful, isn't she?' said Annie, admiring
the little figure. 'Something you can treasure for
always.'

'Will you take me to the hospital later, Mum?'
asked Cherry. 'I'd like to visit Timmy.'

'Of course I will,' said Mrs Stevens. 'Does Annie
want to come too?'

'Yes please,' said Annie.

'Then you'd better stay for tea,' said Cherry's mum affably.

Later that evening, the girls found Timmy's bed in the children's ward. Mrs Rodding was with him. She had been allowed to sleep in the ward too.

Timmy was propped up on numerous starched white pillows. An equally snowy cotton coverlet covered his legs. Although still pale, his eyes sparkled with delight when he saw the giant tube of sweets the girls had brought for him.

'Are you feeling better?' Cherry asked him. Timmy nodded – he was concentrating on the sweets in his hand.

'Yes, he is much better, thank you,' said Mrs Rodding, beaming. 'It's amazing how quickly small children bounce back. He certainly gave us all a fright, though.'

Mrs Rodding was asking the girls a few questions about themselves when her husband arrived.

'Look, Daddy,' said Timmy, holding up the tube of sweets, 'sweeties!'

Mr Rodding laughed. 'I can see you're nearly back to normal,' he said.

Cherry had already offered her thanks to Mrs Rodding for the reward, but now she thanked Mr Rodding also.

'Well, I know my little statuette has found a good home,' said Mr Rodding, with a wink. 'I thought both you girls were exceptional dancers.'

Mr Rodding seemed to have a habit of making

people blush. Annie's cheeks turned as red as Cherry's.

To change the subject, Annie suddenly asked what Señor Bernabo had been doing at the gallery.

'He's our Spanish guest,' she explained. 'Small, thin-faced man. He's my exchange student's uncle.'

'Oh yes,' said Mr Rodding. 'I recall him now. Funny chap. Wanted to sell me a painting. Said he'd brought it over from Spain with him.'

'And did you buy it?' asked Cherry.

'Er no,' said Mr Rodding. 'It was a very nice religious painting, but I just wasn't sure about the source. I like to know exactly where my paintings are coming from.'

'And I suppose Señor Bernabo couldn't tell you very much,' Annie said. 'He can hardly speak a word of English.'

'Oh I wouldn't say that exactly,' said Mr Rodding. 'I mean, he had a very strong accent, but he managed to make himself understood.'

Annie was surprised by this information, and couldn't get it out of her head. Once she and Cherry were back at the Vicarage, and safely out of earshot, she began to talk about the theory she had been forming.

'But that's ridiculous!' cried Cherry. 'Señor Bernabo is a perfectly respectable Spanish gentleman, who is doing research over here. And he's *Gina's uncle!* He couldn't possibly be a criminal!'

'You haven't been as close to him as I have,' said

Annie. 'He's just the sort of person you can imagine being a clever criminal. He probably steals valuable paintings and sells them abroad!'

'Rubbish!' said Cherry. 'It's your imagination getting the better of you again. Remember the ghosts at Miss Rodelle's studio?'

'Look,' said Annie. 'Señor Bernabo is a *very* secretive man. I mean, he pretends at our house that he can't speak a word of English. And yet he manages to have a conversation in English with Mr Rodding about a painting!'

'Perhaps he's just lazy,' Cherry suggested.

'And that day I was in the spare room,' Annie went on, regardless, 'he was absolutely *furious*. He must have something to hide, it's the only explanation.'

'It's *not* the only explanation at all,' said Cherry, with a sigh. 'And what about Gina? I know you're not getting on with her at the moment, and she *is* very vain, but she's no criminal, is she?'

Annie paused. Gina hadn't entered her theories as yet. 'Oh I don't know. She could be his accomplice, or she could be quite innocent!'

'But if he *were* a criminal, she would get to suspect something, surely,' said Cherry.

'I think we've got to keep a careful eye on our Señor,' said Annie. 'And we mustn't let Gina know our suspicions, just in case.'

'It's a waste of effort,' said Cherry. 'I'm sure Gina's uncle isn't mixed up in anything.'

'Well it's a bit of a coincidence that the castle was

broken into, just when he's staying in Shrewsbury, isn't it?' cried Annie.

'There are many other thousands of people in Shrewsbury,' Cherry pointed out. 'It doesn't mean a thing.'

Although she couldn't persuade either Cherry or Pip to her way of thinking, Annie's suspicions of the Bernabos continued to grow. They almost overwhelmed her excitement about her forthcoming birthday. She reached the stage when she simply longed for Gina and her uncle to go home, an event which was due to take place in less than a week's time.

On the morning of her thirteenth birthday, Annie was pleasantly surprised that Gina had bought her a gift. She unwrapped it in the bedroom, after Louisa had come bursting in with her own present for Annie.

'That's lovely, Gina. Thank you!' she said, with genuine pleasure. The present was a Spanish hair-comb, attractively painted.

Gina smiled at her. It was the first time for ages that there had been any good feeling between them. The girls went down to breakfast. As Annie opened her presents from her parents, Gina asked her if she had wanted clothes.

'Oh no!' cried Annie. 'I don't like having clothes for presents. They're too boring.'

Gina couldn't believe her ears. 'But I always have a new dress, a new outfit!'

She stared as Annie opened a two-way radio set, which was just what she had hoped for. Annie squealed with delight and ran to hug her parents.

Her happiness during her special day was infectious. Even at school, Gina seemed to go out of her way to be nice. The only disappointment of the day was that Robbie and Toni turned down Annie's invitation to come to her party. Annie had invited most of her friends from Dance Club, along with her friends' Spanish guests. She tried not to let the disappointment spoil her birthday.

At the party, Gina was in good form, with the circle of other Spanish students around her. In fact, everyone was in high spirits. Mrs Macdonald had laid on a wonderful spread, and afterwards they played silly games, like trying to eat a bar of chocolate with a knife and fork. Then Mr Macdonald rigged up a disco for them. It was all a terrific crush in the Macdonalds' average-sized sitting-room, but this only served to make the atmosphere jollier.

It worked out for the best, Annie thought at bedtime, that Robbie and Toni hadn't been there. She would only have suffered pangs of jealousy every time she looked at them. As she brushed her hair, in her nightshirt, she stared into her dressing-table mirror. *Am I really thirteen?* she asked her reflection. There were signs of change in her face – it was lengthening, along with her nose. She squinted at her profile from both angles and hoped her nose wouldn't get any bigger. *I hope it doesn't get as big as my dad's!* she thought. Then there were the spots — just a few, thank goodness, on her forehead, but spots nonetheless.

She sighed. Would Robbie ever like her again she wondered. Perhaps he would never get over Toni — perhaps they would keep up a long correspondence and eventually get married.

She sighed again. If only you could see into the future. There again, if she didn't have a boyfriend — and she knew no one else but Robbie would ever fit the bill — she would be able to work that much harder at her dancing.

She smiled at herself and put her head on one side. She'd dedicate herself to dancing, that's what she'd do, and one day become a famous ballerina. And then perhaps Robbie would see the mistake he had made all those years ago, and come to her dressing-room with a huge bouquet of red roses ...

Gina interrupted this delightful reverie by coming into the bedroom and jumping into bed.

'I *loved* your party!' she said.

Though annoyed at the interruption of her day-dream, Annie was still on enough of a high to be able to answer Gina in a friendly way.

'It was like being at home,' Gina went on, in raptures. 'Fiesta time! You should come then, Annie.'

It suddenly hit Annie that she would have to make a return visit to Gina's later in the year. It was not a pleasant thought.

'My mother and father and my little brothers and

sisters — we all have enormous paella and then fireworks and games and singing and dancing …'

To Annie's astonishment, Gina burst into floods of tears. There was no doubting they were genuine. Annie went over to her and hugged her, until she had stopped crying violently.

Between sobs, Gina told her how homesick she felt and how much she was missing her parents.

'I'm sorry if I've upset you about "Squib",' said Annie, feeling very guilty. 'Let's be friends again, then perhaps you'll feel a bit happier.'

'Thank you,' said Gina. 'I feel unhappy about "Squib", yes.'

'Well, my offer still stands,' said Annie. 'There's still time to get a couple of rehearsals in before Saturday.'

Gina didn't have to consider for very long. She threw her arms round Annie. 'Yes, I like to come back to Dance Club. I miss you all. And I like to dance in "Squib" on May Day.'

'Brilliant!' Annie declared. 'The others will be so pleased when I tell them. And you haven't much longer to wait until you see your parents.'

Gina's face darkened. 'If only it was tomorrow,' she said.

'But then you couldn't be in the show,' Annie pointed out.

'Yes, apart from that,' said Gina. 'Your family has been very kind. I not being ungrateful.'

'I understand,' said Annie. 'I'm sure I'll be homesick when I come to Spain in October.'

85

'I don't like being with my uncle,' said Gina. 'He is not kind to me, not gentle.'

Annie was not altogether surprised that Gina didn't like Señor Bernabo, though she hadn't thought Gina would let it worry her unduly. But as Gina spoke about her uncle, she became agitated.

Again, Annie wondered about the possibility of criminal activity. Perhaps the uncle was forcing Gina to be involved in something she knew to be wrong. In that case, she knew Gina would be afraid to speak freely. As she suspected, Gina said no more about her uncle. She seemed to snap out of her mood and began chattering once more about the birthday party, and about the forthcoming May Day show.

Annie's friends were delighted when Gina turned up at the Dance Club the next day and Annie explained to them that she had agreed to dance in 'Squib' after all. Most people would have been sheepish, but not Gina. She was soon laughing and joking with everyone.

What was more important, she had lost none of her confidence in her part in the jazz ballet. Other members of the club were still a little rough round the edges, however, so Annie gave them all a 'pep' talk and arranged an extra rehearsal at Cherry's the following evening.

The best part of the day was when Annie was able to tell Clemmie the good news.

'Oh I am pleased,' Clemmie said, smiling. 'I was

beginning to think all my work had been for nothing!'

'I'm pleased too,' said Annie. 'Those costumes deserve to be seen by lots of people – they'll look terrific, I know they will.'

'Well, I shall be there,' said Clemmie. 'D'you want me in the dressing-room?'

'We could do with a bit of help between the two items – there'll be a quick change then. But the rest of the time, you must be up front, to see your handiwork,' Annie replied.

Annie hoped she was forgiven by everyone. Even Robbie had been friendly, now that Toni was back in the show. And Gina was certainly more like her old self – with the exception that she still seemed to be hanging round with Maria quite a lot at school.

At home, Annie was trying to watch Señor Bernabo as much as she could. This was difficult, as he was rarely there and, when he was, he was usually shut up in the spare room.

On Friday it happened that Gina was out, ten-pin bowling with Toni and some of the other Spanish girls, and Señor Bernabo was off doing his research, when Annie had Pip round after their dance classes at Miss Rodelle's.

'Shall we have a look in his room while they're both out of the way?' Annie suggested.

'I don't know,' Pip said nervously. 'You said he was fuming last time he caught you in his room.'

'Oh come on,' said Annie. 'It's easier if there's two of us. You can watch out of the window, in case he comes back. That'll give us plenty of warning.'

Reluctantly, Pip followed Annie to the spare room. She took up her look-out post behind the net curtains, and opened them a crack so she could see out, but couldn't be seen.

'Right,' whispered Annie. 'Let's see what I can find.'

She had a careful look through the drawers and wardrobe, but found only clothes. Under the bed, however, were two suitcases. She pulled them out. They were too heavy to be empty.

'This might be interesting,' she hissed. Pip looked round.

'Hurry up, Annie,' she whispered. 'I don't like this!'

'Just remember, he might be a top class criminal!'

'Or quite innocent!' Pip whispered back.

Both the suitcases were locked.

'Drat!' said Annie.

'He's coming!' hissed Pip urgently.

Annie pushed the cases back under the bed, her heart beginning to thump wildly. As she made for the door, she noticed Pip wasn't following her. She was still peering out at the street.

'What is it?' asked Annie.

'He's gone into the phone box,' said Pip. 'False alarm.'

'We'd better get out of here all the same,' said Annie.

Safely on the landing, Annie suddenly registered what Pip had said.

'Why has he gone in the phone box?' she asked. 'He can use our phone, Mum's told him that!'

Pip shrugged. 'Perhaps it's a private call.'

Annie grinned. 'Follow me!' she said excitedly. 'We're going to listen in – if we're not too late.'

Protesting, Pip was led into Annie's back garden, through the side gate, and then, keeping close to the fence at the side, to a position behind the front hedge.

Crouching down, the two girls were immediately behind the phone box, with the hedge protecting them from being seen.

They strained hard to listen, but it was very difficult to make out anything except odd words.

'I can't make any sense of it, can you?' said Pip.

'Sh!' said Annie. Señor Bernabo was leaving the phone box. He came through the garden gate, and strode down the path, not looking to the right or the left.

The girls shrank into their dim corner, all the same, but he did not see them. He let himself into the house, and the girls ran back round the side and into the rear garden.

'That was a waste of effort!' Pip exclaimed. 'We didn't hear anything important.'

'You're wrong there,' said Annie, sounding very satisfied. 'I learned a great deal. Didn't you notice that he was speaking *in English!*'

'Yes,' said Pip, 'but …'

'Fluent English, at that,' said Annie. 'I'm sure I'm right to be suspicious of our Señor Bernabo!'

9

A Secret Passage

The day before May Day – which fell on a Monday that year – the Dance Club was to go to Shrewsbury Castle for a run-through of the pageant. It was not meant to be a proper dress rehearsal. There wasn't time for all the various groups to rehearse fully. But it would at least give an opportunity to work out entrances and exits and mark positions.

As the band and the gym club were also required, Mrs Race and Mr Farr would be accompanying the children.

Annie's mum drove into the town centre, calling at the Vicarage to pick up Cherry on their way to the castle.

'Aren't you lucky with the weather?' Mrs Macdonald remarked.

It was certainly a very warm start to May. There was not a scrap of cloud in the sky and only the lightest of breezes.

'Are you looking forward to dancing here tomorrow?' Cherry asked Gina, as they drew into the car park beneath the castle.

'I very excited!' Gina exclaimed, peering out of the side window.

'It will be great to do "Squib",' said Annie. 'I'm really looking forward to it. Hope it goes down as well with the audience as "The Little Match Girl" did at Totley.'

'I'm sure it will be a knock-out,' said Cherry. 'It all went fine in the practice yesterday, didn't it? And you were *brilliant*, Gina!'

'Aye,' agreed Annie, as they all got out of the car. 'Oh, I've just had a horrid thought. Maria will be at the castle today, because she's in the band!'

'Oh no,' groaned Cherry. 'I hadn't thought of that!'

'Why you not like Maria?' demanded Gina. 'She very nice girl to me.'

'We just know her better than you do, that's all,' said Annie.

Gina looked rather cross, but said no more as they made their way across the car park and climbed the steps up to the castle. They soon started bumping into other students from Bishop's, including, unfortunately, Maria. Gina, however,

91

looked delighted to see her, and the two of them linked arms and went off together to look round the grounds.

Annie and Cherry exchanged looks.

'They're two of a kind,' said Cherry.

'I don't think Gina's so bad, really,' said Annie. 'Just a bit vain.'

'Mmm,' said Cherry. 'I just hope she behaves herself for the next couple of days. I bet you can't wait for her to go home, can you?'

'It will be nice to have my room back to myself,' said Annie. 'But things haven't been quite so bad since we made friends. I feel quite sorry for her at the moment.'

'Oh look!' said Cherry. 'Robbie and Toni are over there. Shall we go and say hello?'

'Er, nay, it's all right,' said Annie, 'there's plenty of time before we all need to get together. Let's have a look around first.'

The girls met up with Pip quite soon after that, and the three friends wandered happily around the grounds for some time. An arena had been marked out in the centre, and there was already a local marching troupe getting the feel of it.

Closer to the castle itself, a large platform stage had been erected, upon which some members of the school band were setting up chairs and music stands. Mr Farr was organizing the lay-out. When he saw the three girls, he called out to them, and they went over.

'Just the people I wanted to see,' he said. 'The

organizers want to know where you'll be dancing. You've got a choice apparently – on the stage or in the arena.'

'What d'you think?' Annie asked her friends.

'The stage would save our shoes,' said Cherry. 'And it would be easier to go on pointes for "The Little Match Girl".'

'It's a pretty sturdy stage,' said Mr Farr, demonstrating by jumping up and down a few times. 'I think you'd be fine on it.'

'It would be much easier for the staging of "Little Match Girl",' Annie agreed, 'but I don't know about "Squib".'

'No,' said Pip, 'I think "Squib" would look wonderful on grass. And there would be a soft landing too, if anyone falls!'

Cherry laughed. At one point in the dance, they formed a 'human pyramid'. There had been a few tumbles already in the gym, but without injury to anyone.

'No one's going to fall,' Annie chided. 'But I agree – it would be better too, with the audience being able to stand all the way round.

'And there aren't any exits or entrances during the dancing,' said Cherry.

'We only have our black Modern pumps on – the grass won't stain those at all,' added Pip.

So it was settled. 'The Little Match Girl' would be performed at two o'clock on the stage, and 'Squib' immediately afterwards, in the arena. Mr Farr said he would tell the organizers what they'd decided, and told the girls their run-through today was scheduled for 2.30.

'That gives us plenty of time to have a good look around and have our lunch,' said Annie. 'I really want to look inside the castle. I've never been in, have you?'

'No,' said Pip.

'I have,' said Cherry. 'But I was quite small. I don't remember much about it.'

'Come on then,' said Annie. 'I want to go and see the paintings, if we can.'

Annie's wish was granted. There were extra attendants in the gallery, but it was open to the public. The girls made that their first port of call. There were some very large fine old paintings in the rooms, mostly landscapes and portraits. A few were taken from subjects in mythology, and these the girls found the most fascinating.

In the very last chamber, they came across the Degas painting, the likeness of which they'd seen in Mr Rodding's shop. They crowded round and stared at it.

'It *is* better than the copy,' said Annie. 'It's funny how the colours have so much more warmth in the real thing.'

'To think it's worth millions!' Cherry exclaimed. 'It would have been awful if those burglars had got away with it.'

Annie became aware suddenly that one of the attendants was bearing down on them.

'We're making him suspicious,' she hissed to her

94

friends. As they all backed away, and moved on to the next picture, the attendant walked off in another direction.

'They must get very nervous after that break-in,' whispered Pip.

'When are we going to eat our packed lunch?' asked Cherry.

'Oh you're nay hungry already!' Annie exclaimed. 'We haven't looked round the rest of the castle yet.'

'Come on then,' said Cherry. 'Let's get it over with.'

They went back to the ground floor of the building and wandered through rooms where military treasures, weapons and suits of armour were on display.

'The knights of old must have been quite tiny,' Cherry remarked, measuring herself up against a shiny suit of armour. 'I wouldn't be able to fit in this one.'

'I'd love to clamber inside one, wouldn't you?' said Annie, looking round at the empty room. 'And peer out of the visor!'

'Don't even think of it!' exclaimed Pip, frowning at her impulsive friend.

An attendant appeared in the doorway just then, preventing any possibility of mischief.

The girls moved on, until they reached the far end of the castle. They hadn't seen another person since the attendant.

'Everyone's outside on a lovely day like this,' Pip remarked.

'Oh look,' said Annie. 'That bit's roped off. I wonder why?'

A large **NO ENTRY** sign was hanging on the red rope, barring their access to a further door, which itself was marked, **PRIVATE**.

'I wonder what's through there?' said Annie. 'I bet it's something exciting, don't you?'

'I doubt it,' said Cherry. 'It's probably just a store-room, where the cleaners keep all their cleaning stuff.'

'Och!' Annie wrinkled her nose in disgust. 'You're so unromantic, Cherry!'

'It could be dangerous,' Pip remarked. 'You know like the Tower used to be!'

'Well,' said Annie. 'Whatever it is, it's very mysterious. Who wants to explore with me?'

Both her friends shook their heads emphatically.

'Where's your sense of adventure?' Annie demanded. 'Well, I'm going to try the door, and if it's unlocked, I'm going in. With you or without you.'

'That attendant might come back,' said Pip. 'We really shouldn't, Annie!'

'Don't be such a wimp,' said Annie. She was quite determined to explore further and her friends could see it would be useless to try and deter her.

Annie stepped over the rope and walked the few paces to the door. She tried the handle but it was locked.

Cherry and Pip breathed a sigh of relief.

'What a shame,' said Annie, sounding very

disappointed. She turned to face her friends, moving to one side of the door, and rested her back against the stone wall.

She felt one of the stone blocks move in slightly behind her, and at the same time, there was a rumbling noise in the floor between her and her friends.

All three of them stared in disbelief as a section of the wooden floor slowly gave way, leaving an opening about a metre square.

'What on earth's going on?' Annie squealed. She twizzled round and looked at the stone wall. One of the blocks had definitely been depressed.

'This must operate a lever somewhere,' she said, 'which opens that hatch in the floor.'

The other two had tiptoed forward and were staring down the opening.

'There are steps doing downwards – quite a long way, by the look of it,' whispered Cherry.

'How exciting,' said Pip.

'This is better than getting through the door!' cried Annie. 'What amazing luck, to have found the right bit of wall!'

By now, her friends were as intrigued as Annie and they didn't need any persuading at all to follow her down the steps. It was quite a long way down to the bottom.

There was just enough light left there to see a dim passageway leading off from the stone steps.

'Wherever does it lead to?' cried Annie.

'We can't go any further,' said Cherry. 'Not

without torches.'

'No,' agreed Pip. 'It's impossible to see anything ahead. It would be pointless.'

'OK,' Annie agreed, a little reluctantly. 'We must bring torches tomorrow. We can explore it in the morning!'

'Brilliant!' said Pip. 'It will be a wonderful May Day adventure.

The friends clambered back up the steps and were about to emerge through the hatch, when they heard the unmistakable sound of footsteps approaching.

Annie, who was on the highest step, quickly closed the hatch. They heard a slight rumble as the stone block in the wall moved back into position. As they were plunged into blackness, it flashed through Annie's mind that they might have sealed themselves in. Perhaps there was no way of opening the hatch again from the inside!

With that terrifying thought, she tried to stay stock still. The footsteps – two sets by the sound of it – had come over to a point very close to the roped-off area. It must be two attendants, Annie thought.

At first, her mind didn't take in what she was hearing, but then, with a shock, she realized she was listening to a conversation in Spanish. And not only that, but she recognized the speakers! One was Gina, and the other Señor Bernabo.

They were arguing, that was plain, but the words that were coming from Señor Bernabo were much too fast for Annie to have any hope of understanding.

The only thing she *did* make out, was when Gina said, 'Please don't!' in a very high frightened voice.

There was the sound of a slap, followed by Gina's crying and another torrent of angry words from her uncle.

Annie had a strong impulse to burst out of the hatch and tell Señor Bernabo what she thought of him, but a feeling of caution stopped her. She wondered what he was doing here at the castle and what the argument was all about.

After a few more minutes, the pair moved away, and the room became silent once more.

'D'you think it's safe to go up now?' whispered Pip.

'Cross your fingers we can get the hatch open!' said Annie.

She and Cherry found a ring in the wood panel and pulled hard, but it wouldn't budge.

'Oh, no!' groaned Pip. 'Don't say we're stuck here!'

Annie was feeling all round the panel blindly. 'There must be a way of opening it from this side,' she said, trying not to panic.

More footsteps echoed through their hiding-place, and they were forced to stay still once more. This time, it probably was an attendant, as the footsteps did a tour of the room and then departed.

'Oh hurry up and get us out!' gasped Pip. 'I feel as if I'm suffocating!'

'I'm doing my best,' said Annie, using her fingers as eyes once more.

At last, they encountered a small metal lever – she knew it was metal because it was so cold to the touch. She tried to move it in all directions, but without success. Just as she was about to give up, Cherry suggested she tried pushing it in. She did this, and the rumbling noise began as before.

How welcome the daylight was that streamed down the steps as the hatch started to move downwards! And how eagerly the girls scrambled up into the room!

'Let's get out of here!' cried Pip, moving away.

'We can't leave the hatch open!' said Annie, already investigating the stone block in the wall. There was no way, however, that anyone could fit their fingers around the sunken stone to pull it back.

'We'll *have* to leave it open!' said Cherry. 'Come on, Annie. We'd better get out of here before that attendant comes back on his rounds!'

'Wait a minute,' said Annie. 'There *must* be a way of closing it. If we manage it, it can be our secret. I don't suppose anyone else has been down there for ages.'

'Do you really think so?' cried Pip.

'It's very well concealed,' said Annie. 'We could be the first people to stumble across it in centuries!'

When she continued to feel the wall and floor for any irregularities, Cherry and Pip joined in the search. It was Cherry who found the secret in the

100

end. Another stone block to the right of the first moved inwards under the pressure of her hands, and the hatch creaked upwards.

'Success!' Annie exclaimed.

They crossed the rope boundary and stared at the floor. There was no trace of a hatch to be seen. The wooden blocks fitted together like a jigsaw.

'It's amazing!' breathed Cherry.

'What did you make of the conversation we overheard?' asked Annie, suddenly remembering the awful row they'd been witness to.

'Was it Gina?' asked Pip.

'Yes, and her uncle,' said Annie.

'He sounded very angry with her,' said Pip. 'And very rough. Wasn't that a slap he gave her?'

'It sounded like it,' said Cherry. 'Poor Gina. I wonder why she'd upset him so much?'

'I don't know,' said Annie thoughtfully. 'But it's mighty suspicious that Señor Bernabo is lurking about the castle, isn't it? I'm sure he's up to no good!'

'If he *is* a thief,' said Cherry slowly, 'does that mean Gina has guessed or something and that's what the row's about?'

'Gina could be in terrible danger, if that's true,' cried Pip. 'Whatever can we do?'

'She may have known all along!' said Annie. 'We just can't tell, can we?'

'No,' said Cherry, shaking herself. 'We're getting carried away. Finding a secret passage and all that! We've got to come down to earth again. Señor

101

Bernabo's just a moody old man. He *can't* be a criminal.'

'I hope you're right,' said Pip. 'But I really didn't like the way he was treating Gina.'

'It would be much easier to try and protect Gina if she didn't keep going off with Maria,' said Annie, 'but short of kidnapping her ...'

'No, there's not a lot we can do except stay wide awake,' said Pip. 'And Cherry's probably right. We're letting our imaginations get the better of us!'

· 10 ·

Strange Hiding-place

Although they were feeling ravenous, the girls
decided to look for Gina before starting their
picnic, to see if she was all right. They came across
her, not as they had expected, with Maria, but with
Sam, Robbie and Antonia. This made Annie feel ill
at ease. She had been trying to avoid contact with
Robbie and Toni as much as possible.

'There you are, Gina!' Cherry cried in a friendly
tone.

'We thought you might like to eat lunch with us,'
added Pip.

Gina's face bore the tell-tale marks of tears but
she forced a smile.

'Let's all sit together, then,' urged Robbie. 'Toni

and I haven't had ours yet.'

How that *Toni and I* stuck in Annie's gullet! Every time she saw them together they looked even more chummy than the last! She forced her attention to focus on Gina. She certainly looked pale and unhappy. Perhaps she had come to Toni for comfort.

Reluctantly, Annie sat down with the others and opened her pack of sandwiches. She tucked in hungrily, as did her friends. Looking up after she had eaten every last crumb, Annie was mortified to see that Toni had only nibbled at *her* sandwiches, and was putting whole chunks back in her lunch-box.

'Aren't you hungry?' Sam asked her.

Toni laughed a high-pitched laugh.

'Robbie knows I eat like a little mouse.'

Annie quickly hid her empty wrappings in her bag and started talking about the run-through.

'There'll be a few things we'll need to change in "The Little Match Girl",' she said. 'Pip, I thought we'd have you coming in at the back right of the stage. There's a big speaker there you can hide behind until it's time for the grandmother to appear.'

'Good idea,' said Pip.

'That means the angels will have to enter from the right too,' said Annie, 'which will be a bit different from how we've rehearsed it.'

'Never mind,' said Cherry. 'We'll soon get it straight when we've walked it through.'

'Where do we come in for "Squib"?' asked Toni.

'There's only one way into the arena,' said Annie. 'The rest is roped off.'

'The arena!' Robbie said. 'I didn't think we'd be doing it there!'

'The arena! Pff!' cried Toni. 'I want to dance on the stage!'

Gina was shaken out of her day-dreams by this news.

'No, no, no!' she exclaimed. 'I will not dance on this damp English grass!'

'It's not damp today, Gina,' Annie remonstrated with her, as mildly as she could.

'It will be tomorrow!' said Gina, quite illogically. She was beginning to look upset and Annie was desperately trying to think of something to pacify her.

'We thought we'd get a much bigger audience for an event in the arena,' she said hopefully. 'Masses of people can stand all the way round the arena, you see.'

'Bigger audience?' Gina repeated. She looked at Toni.

'The grass is not so damp,' Toni said.

'And more people will get a clear view of you, in the round,' Annie pressed on, even more hopefully.

'Then we will dance on the grass,' said Gina, her temper subsiding.

Annie breathed an inward sigh of relief and stood up, unable to bear the tensions any longer.

'Stay here,' she said. 'I'm going to scout round for the others and tell them to meet up here.'

'D'you want me to come with you?' asked Cherry.

'No, it's all right, thanks,' said Annie. She quite fancied the idea of a little walk on her own to clear her head.

Once she'd rounded up the rest of the gang and sent them off to where the others were sitting, Annie discovered she'd still got some time to kill. She knew Cherry and Pip would be keeping an eye on Gina. Somehow she felt reluctant to go back just yet. Being in the company of Robbie and Toni for long made her feel uncomfortable. And she was still feeling very excited about the secret passageway.

On an impulse, she headed back into the castle, for another quick look at the far chamber where they had found it. It was almost to convince herself that it was really there, and that she had not been dreaming.

As before, by the time she reached the far end there were no visitors about, and no sign of an attendant. She stood by the barrier rope, staring first at the floor, and then at the wall. But however hard she looked, no sign of either the hatch or the moving stones became visible.

She thought about trying it out again, but this might be tempting fate. Then another idea crossed her mind, which made her grin to herself. She scurried back to the entrance to the chamber to check if anyone was about. When it was all clear, she came back to one of the suits of armour on display and took a deep breath.

Sixty seconds later she was inside it, looking out through a slit in the visor! *Now I know what it feels like to be a knight!* she thought, *or maybe a sardine in a tin!* The armour was a pretty tight fit. She could feel the helmet pressing down on the top of her head. Feeling uncomfortable, she had just decided to get out of the metal suit, when the sound of footsteps made her freeze.

Peering through the slit, she saw two men move into the chamber. With a shock, she recognized Señor Bernabo. The second man was unknown to her, but he was English, not Spanish.

The men were murmuring together in low tones, which Annie strained to hear. She saw Señor Bernabo look at his watch. Then they moved across towards the rope barrier, just out of Annie's range of sight. Listening intently, she caught the words 'in the store' and 'guards' but that was all. It was very frustrating. Annie felt sure they were plotting something. How she wished she could see what they were doing over by the barrier! There was no rumbling noise to indicate they had found the secret passageway. That was a great relief!

She heard someone else come into the chamber. It was the attendant. Señor Bernabo and his colleague came back into view, moving towards her and the rest of the display of armour and swords. Annie was filled with terror, in case one of them looked straight into her eyes. They were the only part of her that wasn't hidden.

Señor Bernabo was walking straight towards her! With the small amount of movement that the helmet allowed her, she shook her hair, which fortunately she had not tied back that morning, over her face. She could see hardly anything through the thick dark mass. And luckily, neither could Señor Bernabo. He quickly moved on to look at the next suit of armour.

Annie's nose began to itch violently. She wished all three of them would hurry up and go away. She was thoroughly tired of her prank by now, and conscious that it must be nearly time for the Dance Club's run-through. Her friends would wonder what had happened to her!

She was desperate to scratch her nose and get her hair off her face. She couldn't tell exactly how close any of the men were to her now, so didn't dare move a muscle.

At last came the welcome sound of receding footsteps. But were there three sets? She wasn't really sure. She held her breath, listening for any further sound in the chamber. When she was quite satisfied she was alone, she extricated herself as quickly as she could from the armour and rubbed her nose hard.

Breaking into a run, she made her way through the castle, hoping she wouldn't bump into Señor Bernabo. There was no sign of him, however, and she got to the stage in the grounds without further mishap.

'Where on earth have you been?' cried Cherry. 'Everyone else has been here for ages!'

'Can't explain now,' said Annie breathlessly. 'Sorry, anyway.'

She caught sight of Gina's scowling face coming towards her.

'Cherry said I must come here at 2.30. You have not started "The Little Match Girl" yet. Why not I go with Maria until "Squib"?'

'But Gina,' Cherry said. 'I explained to you, we need *all* the club members here. You might be needed off-stage.'

'That's right,' said Pip. 'And we don't know for sure how long the walk through of The Match Girl will take.'

'Not long, I hope,' said Mr Farr, appearing at the side of the platform, looking at his watch. 'You've wasted nearly ten minutes already. You're only allowed until 2.45. Then a further five minutes in the arena.'

'Oh no,' groaned Annie. 'Well, let's stop arguing and get on with it, shall we?'

Annie had no time during the following ten minutes to even *think* about her further encounter with Señor Bernabo, let alone tell her friends about it.

Luckily, Annie had already formed a good mental plan of the exits and entrances for 'The Little Match Girl', so the run-through went perfectly smoothly. 'Squib' should have been easier, as they all entered and exited together. The only problem was knowing which way to face.

Gina was in an argumentative mood. When Annie suggested they faced away from the castle, she disagreed. A vote had to be taken, wasting valuable minutes. When Annie's suggestion was carried, Gina's face became even longer. Annie realized that she was in quite an unstable mood. She just hoped the Spanish girl didn't do anything silly, like refuse to take part again. Annie went out of her way to be nice to her. It wasn't just a pretence either. She really did feel very sorry for her now that she had seen how badly her uncle was treating her.

At last everything was sorted out and the Dance Club dispersed, after being told their performance times for the following day.

Annie couldn't wait to tell Pip and Cherry about what had happened to her, but had to be patient, as Gina remained with them from then on, until Mrs Macdonald picked them up not long after.

Luckily Gina gradually regained her natural cheerfulness, and began talking about the 'lovely costumes' they would be wearing the next day for 'Squib'.

Annie felt pleased that Gina would not be on her own with her uncle again that evening. She watched carefully for any reaction in her at the supper table, but she showed none when her uncle sat down, last as always.

Once Señor Bernabo's eyes were safely fastened on his meal, Annie had a good look at him. There

110

was certainly a shifty look about his face. If only she could tell Cherry and Pip her latest suspicions.

She decided to make a phone call to Cherry. It would be too dangerous from the house. She would use the phone box in the street.

Making an excuse about 'needing some fresh air', Annie nipped out to the box just outside the house, hoping no one would look out of the front window.

She dialled Cherry's number and quickly told her what had happened.

'They were "casing the joint", I'm sure!' Annie cried.

'What makes you so sure?' Cherry asked.

'Well, their manner. They looked really suspicious. And the way they were whispering. And what they said …'

'I thought you couldn't hear what they said?' Cherry reminded her.

'Not most of it,' Annie admitted. 'But I heard "in the store" and "guards" …'

'There could be a perfectly innocent explanation for all of this,' said Cherry. 'It doesn't add up to criminal intentions …'

'I know that,' said Annie, a little sulkily. 'I mean, I know we couldn't go to the police yet and expect them to do anything.'

'Exactly,' said Cherry. 'The more I think about it, the more unlikely it seems.'

'But you didn't see how suspicious they looked!' cried Annie.

'Someone might have said the same of you, if

they'd found you hiding in that suit of armour!'
Cherry said, chuckling.

Deflated, Annie said goodbye to her friend. At
least the expedition down the passageway with
torches was still on. Cherry had sounded quite
excited about it.

Feeling thoughtful, Annie returned to her
bedroom, where Gina was lying on one of the twin
beds, writing up her diary.

'It's not long till you go home now,' Annie
remarked, when she had finished and closed up
her book.

'No,' said Gina. 'I count the days.'

'Will your uncle travel all the way home with
you?' Annie asked.

'No,' Gina replied. 'He is not going back on the
coach with us.'

'I see,' said Annie. 'Has he enjoyed doing his
research here, d'you think?'

She was waiting for Gina to show signs of
suspicion at this question, but instead she looked
angry.

'I don't want to talk of my uncle,' she said.

'Has he upset you?' Annie asked, innocently.

'Si, very much,' said Gina, her eyes brimming
with tears.

'Don't worry, Gina,' Annie said, putting her arms
round her. 'You'll soon be back with your parents.
Just keep away from him till then.'

'It's not so easy,' said Gina. 'If he tell my father I
have been rude, my father very angry with me.'

'Does your father believe everything he says?'

'Si. *Everything*. My father fears him, I think. His oldest brother. Head of the family since my grandfather has died.'

'And was your grandfather like him?' asked Annie.

'Like my uncle?' Gina began to laugh. 'Oh no, my grandfather was very kind and very fat. More like my *father*!'

The girls fell silent as they heard Señor Bernabo climb the stairs and go into his room. He carried an unpleasant atmosphere around with him, which Annie could sense now by a sort of prickling at the back of her head.

'Let's talk about "Squib",' said Gina.

'Right,' said Annie. 'It's all going to happen tomorrow.'

'Mañana,' whispered Gina.

Underground

Annie had a lot to think about when she woke next morning. She still felt thoroughly convinced that Señor Bernabo was the art thief who had already made an attempt to break in at Shrewsbury Castle. But what she couldn't make up her mind about was whether Gina knew anything about his criminal activities or not. If Gina did, Annie could well understand that she'd be too scared to expose him.

Then of course, there was the pageant. It was a wonderful opportunity for the Dance Club to display their talents and get a name for themselves – if they danced well.

And finally, there was the most exciting prospect of exploring the secret passageway.

While Gina was in the bathroom, Annie hid her most powerful torch and her radio set in the bottom of her dance bag, laying her costumes for the pageant on top.

'You pack already?' Gina said cheerfully, coming back into the room.

'I like to get organized,' said Annie, smiling back at her. 'Well, this is the day! Have you looked outside? The sun's lovely!'

Gina parted the curtains. Sunlight streamed through the gap.

'My costume will sparkle like fire!' Gina exclaimed.

'And we won't get wet feet,' said Annie. 'You've been really lucky with the weather while you've been here. It can be cold and wet in April and May.'

'Still much colder than Spain,' said Gina, pretending to shiver.

Annie laughed. She had got quite used to having Gina around. If it weren't for her awful uncle, Annie might not mind staying in Spain with her too much.

The pageant didn't officially open until one o'clock, but participants were allowed to go and set up from ten o'clock onwards. Annie had arranged to meet her friends at the castle at about 10.30, so they would have plenty of time for their exploring. The only problem was Gina.

Annie suggested to her mother that she brought Gina down later in the morning, but Mrs Macdonald was too busy to make two journeys. She insisted that Gina must come at 10.30, along with Annie.

'It would be a bit rude to go off without her, anyway,' said Mrs Macdonald.

In the car, Annie racked her brains to think of a way of getting rid of Gina. She even found herself hoping that Maria would arrive early too!

Then she felt really guilty. The friends were supposed to be keeping a watchful eye on Gina, to protect her from her horrid uncle. But how could they explore the secret passageway if Gina stayed with them?

As she and Gina walked into the grounds, Cherry and Pip came running up to them.

'All set?' asked Pip excitedly.

Annie grinned.

'We'd better take our costumes to the dressing-room first,' said Cherry.

'Good idea,' said Gina. 'Then we can walk around together.'

The three friends exchanged horrified looks. They trooped off to the castle entrance glumly. Here they were stopped by two security guards in uniform. The castle had been closed to members of the public while the pageant was taking place. Annie and her friends had to give the men their names, and which group they belonged to. One of the guards checked the names against a list before giving them passes for the day and directions to their dressing-room.

'They seem to be taking a lot of care,' Cherry

remarked, as they made their way to the dressing-room.

'They're bound to have tightened up security since that break-in,' said Annie.

When they found the dressing-room, it had **Bishop's Dance Club** and **The Minettes** on the door. They were the first arrivals.

'Who are the Minettes?' asked Pip.

'I think they're the marching troupe,' said Annie. 'Quite young – only seven or eight.'

'I don't suppose they'll arrive until this afternoon,' said Cherry.

The girls left their bags (with their torches and Annie's two-way radio hidden in them) and went back out into the grounds. Annie was keeping an eye open for Señor Bernabo – she felt sure he would pop up sooner or later, but there was no sign of him yet.

As the friends strolled around, watching various people setting up stalls and activities, they longed to get back to their secret passage. But Gina showed no sign of wanting to leave them.

They passed several craft stalls, with goods made from wood and pottery being organized into displays for the afternoon. There were a couple of side-stalls for children, with cheap toys, garish snakes on sticks and candy-floss for sale. Then they came to rather larger stands, which as yet remained empty.

Annie caught sight of a familiar face setting up one of these.

'Mr Rodding!' she called out.

He returned her greeting and the girls ran across to him.

'What are you doing here?' she asked.

'How can you ask?' he exclaimed. 'Don't you know I'm your club's number one fan? I wouldn't miss your performance this afternoon for the world.'

As Gina smiled radiantly at him, Annie suddenly remembered they hadn't been introduced.

'Mr Rodding,' she said, 'this is Gina Bernabo.'

'Hello there,' he said. 'Hope you're enjoying your stay in England?'

'Yes, thank you,' said Gina politely.

Annie saw a flicker of interest in Mr Rodding's eyes – was he remembering Gina's uncle's visit to his shop?

'So, why are you building this stall if you're just going to be in the audience?' Annie asked mischievously.

Mr Rodding grinned. 'You've caught me out,' he said. 'We have to mix business with pleasure sometimes, you know.'

'Are you going to have some of your pictures for sale then?' asked Cherry.

'Yes, that's the idea,' he replied. 'Including your favourite!'

'The Degas?' asked Annie.

'Yes. What a shame you won't get to see the original today. I hear it's been taken out of the gallery and put into the security vault for the day. To be on the safe side, I guess.'

'It's OK,' said Cherry. 'We went to see it yesterday when the gallery was still open to the public.'

'Oh good,' said Mr Rodding. 'Well, good luck with your performance!'

'Thanks!' the girls chorused, as they moved away.

Annie stopped in her tracks, almost as soon as she'd begun. A stallholder just along from Mr Rodding had just arrived and was getting out of his van. She gripped Cherry's arm.

'That's him,' she whispered urgently.

'Who?' Cherry whispered back.

Gina looked round at them.

'Just a man I've seen before,' Annie said quickly. She turned back to Mr Rodding. 'Do you know that man?' she asked, pointing discreetly at him.

'Why yes, he's an antiques dealer. Based in Shrewsbury. Why?'

'Oh, nothing. I just thought I'd seen him before,' said Annie.

'Well you probably have. He has a big showroom in the town.'

'Thanks, Mr Rodding,' said Annie, rejoining her friends.

'What was that all about?' asked Cherry.

Annie elbowed her and frowned. Cherry took the hint and stayed quiet.

Just when the friends were beginning to give up hope of ever getting to the secret passageway, Maria turned up.

'Hi, Gina!' she said. 'The band's arrived. Want to come round with us for a bit?'

Gina looked flattered that Maria had come looking for her and went off with her quite readily.

'Great!' squealed Pip. 'Now we can get started.'

'I thought she was going to stick with us all morning!' cried Cherry, as they raced towards the castle entrance, to retrieve the torches and radio. 'Who was your mystery man, by the way?'

'It was the man I saw with Señor Bernabo when I was in the suit of armour!' cried Annie. 'So now we know he's a dealer. Interesting!'

In great excitement, the girls showed their passes to the guards and walked through the part of the ground floor where all the performers had been housed.

Annie suddenly stopped short. 'We haven't been thinking straight!' she said to them. 'What's the use of a two-way radio of we're *all* underground!'

'Well, we don't have to use it!' said Cherry.

'But I really want to try it out!' cried Annie. 'And it's a safety measure. Suppose we got trapped down there.'

'But we know how to open the hatch now,' said Pip. 'It wouldn't be fair for the one who had to stay above ground.' Her face showed her anxiety in case she should be this unfortunate person.

'We'll have to draw lots,' said Annie firmly.

As they reached their dressing-room, they were surprised to find Sam sitting in there, messing with his camera.

'Hi,' he said cheerfully. 'Thought I'd get here early to take some photos.'

'What a stroke of luck!' cried Pip.

Annie shot her a warning glance.

'We can tell Sam, surely?' said Pip. 'Especially as Robbie and Toni aren't around yet.'

'Tell me what?' asked Sam, looking puzzled. 'Are you lot up to something again?'

Annie thought they'd better tell him now. She had to admit he would make it easier to use the radio. And Sam was always trustworthy. After Pip had explained everything, Sam agreed eagerly to their request.

'A secret passage, you say?' he cried.

'Keep your voice down,' Annie begged. 'I'm sorry you can't come underground with us.'

'That's OK,' said Sam evenly. 'But I'd like to see the hatch opened up!'

'That'll be all right,' said Annie, 'but don't hang about in that room. It might look suspicious.'

'No, I won't,' Sam agreed. 'I'll get on with my photography outside.'

The four friends moved out of the area where all the dressing-rooms were. They were soon walking towards the other end of the castle.

'It's deserted, isn't it?' said Pip.

'Yes,' said Annie, her eyes dancing. 'Couldn't be better for us. No attendants on duty, or anything.'

'Well, there wouldn't be,' Cherry pointed out, 'when the castle's closed to the public.'

Once they reached the final chamber, Annie

121

challenged Sam to see if he could find out how to open the secret hatch. They wouldn't give him any clues, even when he begged.

'Oh come on!' he pleaded. 'Don't leave me in suspense.'

Giggling, the girls depressed the stone in the wall, which operated the hatch.

Sam's eyes widened in wonder as the hole appeared in the floor at his feet. He peered down at the steps which led down from it.

'Cool!' he said. 'How far d'you reckon the passage goes?'

'We've no idea,' said Pip. 'It was too dark to see last time.'

Annie and Cherry nipped down the steps, while Pip showed Sam all the secret mechanisms. They flashed their torches along the passageway.

'It seems to go a long way!' Annie called back to Pip excitedly. Pip scurried down the steps, saying a quick goodbye to Sam, who – now rather reluctantly – made his way out of the chamber, with Annie's radio tucked into his denim jacket pocket.

Before the girls had gone very far at all, they saw a massive oak door to their right. Curious, Annie stopped to see if she could open it. It was unlocked, but it took the three of them to push it open. Once open, it stayed jammed, and couldn't be closed again.

'I wonder where this leads to,' said Annie, shining her torch ahead. It was a wider tunnel than the main one, but they quickly saw it came to a dead-end.

'If I've got my bearings right, the room on the other side of the No Entry sign should be on our right now,' said Annie. She shone her torch carefully along that wall. There was more recent brickwork at one point, where another doorway had been filled in.

'There must be a cellar under the No Entry room, which this door must have led to,' said Annie. The other two crowded round her to look.

'You'd make a good detective,' laughed Cherry.

A sudden thought struck Annie. 'Perhaps it's the security vault on the other side of this wall!' she cried.

'Could be,' said Cherry. 'It's a good job they've bricked up the old door in that case.'

A phrase of Señor Bernabo's came back into Annie's mind. 'In the store,' she whispered.

'What?' said Cherry.

'Gina's uncle – he said "in the store". What if he meant the vault? The painting was in the vault! He was standing right in front of the entrance to it, if I'm right!'

'Wow,' said Pip. 'It all adds up really, doesn't it, Cherry?'

Even Cherry had to admit it did.

'Wouldn't it be awful,' said Annie, turning pale, 'if he had found this secret passageway?'

'Let's hope it's just our secret,' said Cherry. 'You did remember to shut the hatch behind you, when you came down, didn't you Pip?'

'Oh no!' groaned Pip. 'With all the excitement, I

forgot! I'll go and do it straight away!'

She rushed off with her torch.

'Why is Pip always so scatty?' sighed Annie.

'Well, no harm done,' said Cherry. 'There's no one about.'

'If Señor Bernabo tried to get into the vault from above, we'd hear him from here and be able to warn Sam,' said Annie, when Pip had returned.

'All clear,' said Pip.

'I don't think he'd get in,' said Cherry. 'Vaults usually have tremendously thick metal doors and that, don't they?'

'You're right,' said Annie. 'There was no sign of him about. He's probably waiting till the Degas is put back on display.'

'Much more likely,' said Cherry. 'I just wish we had something definite to take to the police.'

The girls retraced their steps to the main tunnel and followed it for several hundred yards.

'It's a really long tunnel,' Cherry remarked.

'Shall we get in touch with Sam and report our progress so far?' Annie suggested.

The girls agreed, so they paused while Annie took out her radio set, and proceeded to call Sam.

'Potholers calling Lord Lichfield. Over!' she said gleefully.

'Who's Lord Lichfield?' asked Cherry.

'Sh!' Annie warned.

'A famous photographer, of course,' hissed Pip.

Sam's crackly voice came over the radio, faintly. 'Lichfield to potholers. What is your position? Over.'

124

Annie told him all they'd seen so far and ended with: 'Further report to follow at end of tunnel. Over and out!'

Feeling really pleased with her radio set, Annie led her friends further along the tunnel.

At last it opened out into what seemed to be a natural cave, formed in the sandstone rock. It wasn't totally natural, however. Along one side of it ran a tough metal grille, and beyond that, wooden slatting and a door. The grille was padlocked, so it was impossible for them to get to the door. But it *was* possible for them to peer through the grille, between a couple of the slats which didn't quite meet, and see daylight outside.

'I wonder where we are?' said Annie.

Cherry, who had the best view, answered, 'It looks like we're above the back of the railway station! What d'you think?'

Annie and Pip each looked from Cherry's spyhole, and came to the same conclusion. Then they flashed their torches around the cave. There was a heap of tarpaulins in one corner, and in another, a large object with a dust-sheet over it. Annie removed the sheet.

'Wow!' gasped Cherry.

Under it was a beautiful bronze statue of a horse.

'This must be worth a lot of money,' said Pip, walking round it.

'Whatever is it doing here?' asked Cherry.

Annie was beginning to feel nervous. 'Someone must know about the tunnel,' she whispered.

'It could be the castle staff. This could be used as a store-room,' Cherry suggested. 'That's why it's all padlocked.'

'I don't know,' said Annie. 'I've a funny feeling about it.'

There was a slight movement in the corner where the tarpaulins were heaped.

'What was that?' hissed Pip.

'Shall we look?' whispered Cherry.

'No,' said Annie. 'Might be rats! Let's get out of here!'

Pip and Cherry made no objection to following Annie back along the tunnel. All three of them felt nervous now, and eager to get back to the hatch.

They were just abreast of the tunnel to their left, when a clanging noise reverberated from back down the passageway. All three of them froze, and stopped breathing, to listen better.

What they heard made their hearts quicken alarmingly. Heavy footsteps were coming along the tunnel from the cave end.

Would there be time to reach the hatch? Even if there were, the mechanism was quite noisy. Whoever was coming this way would be alerted to their presence.

Annie's mind whirled. There was only one thing for it. She grabbed Pip's and Cherry's hands and pulled them around the open oak door. She pushed them in the gap between the door and the wall, and quickly followed herself.

Thank goodness it's a huge door, Annie thought to

herself. It was also fortunate all three girls were so slim.

The footsteps were getting closer. As they drew level with the door, then entered the same branch of the tunnel, the girls hardly dared breathe.

Annie prayed the intruders wouldn't try to close the door behind them, or flash one of their torches into their hiding-place! But no, the men – Annie could see they were men – moved further along and shone their beams on the bricked-up doorway the girls had studied earlier.

It must be a way into the vault, like I guessed, thought Annie.

The men started taping bundles to the wall.

'Will anyone hear it?' said one, whose voice Annie instantly recognized as Señor Bernabo's.

'Doubt it,' came the gruff answer. 'The castle walls are so damned thick. And the brass band's making a hell of a racket outside!'

As this man laid a flex from the bundles, back along the branch passage, Annie realized with a shock what they were doing. Both men retreated out of sight, into the main tunnel.

Annie smelt burning. They must have lit the fuse! When they blew up the wall into the vault, would the friends be in the way of the blast? Annie knew the other two couldn't possibly have seen what was going on. She pushed back, shrinking as far from the explosives as she possibly could. As she squashed into them, she could hear faint murmurs of protest.

Now she could see the flame travelling up the fuse towards its target. Annie turned her face away and brought one arm up over her head ...

· 12 ·

Flash, Bang, Wallop

What followed was like the worst thunderstorm Annie could imagine, minus the rain. The explosion, which must have come as a complete shock to Cherry and Pip, left all three girls trembling with fear. Dust and bits of masonry were blown at them, even in their sheltered position.

Annie took the worst of the blast, but though she was hurt on her leg and shoulder by flying debris, she knew she hadn't been badly injured.

Otherwise, the choking dust was the main problem. They all started coughing – they couldn't help themselves, but tried to muffle it in their clothing.

Annie guessed, even before she was able to turn

her head and look, that the men had gone straight in through the hole they had blown. They would be too busy to notice the girls spluttering, hopefully.

When her eyes, and the dust, cleared, there was no sign of them in the passageway. In urgent whispers, she told her friends what had happened.

'Why don't we run for it?' she whispered. 'We might make it back to the hatch before they hear us.'

Her heart in her mouth, Annie led them back towards the main tunnel, picking her way over debris. They had nearly reached it when she heard something. She stopped and put out a restraining arm.

'There's someone coming!' Footsteps could be heard advancing down the main tunnel, from the cave end. And they were pretty close!

'Get back. Quick!' Annie hissed, turning.

They scurried back behind the door.

'The radio,' Cherry croaked. 'Tell Sam.'

Annie whipped it out and hoped the oak door would conceal her whispers from whoever was coming closer. Luckily, she got through to Sam straight away.

'Listen carefully, Sam. We're trapped in the branch off the main tunnel. Bernabo and accomplice have blown their way into the vault. They'll be out soon with the Degas. And someone else is …'

Here she had to break off, for safety's sake, as the footsteps had drawn level with the door.

To her intense surprise, what she heard next was girls' voices. Gina's and Maria's voices, to be precise.

'Whatever's been going on here?' said Maria.

'I do not know,' said Gina. She sounded genuinely shocked. At last, Annie could entirely believe in her innocence. She had obviously no inkling of what her uncle was up to.

Annie's mind careered about like a helter-skelter. What on earth were Gina and Maria doing here? She could only think they had followed the friends down the steps, in the time Pip had forgotten to close the hatch. But why hadn't they bumped into them before now, in that case?

Then Annie remembered going into the branch first. Gina and Maria could have shot past along the main tunnel, without them seeing. And the movement under the tarpaulin! That had been no rat! It must have been Gina and Maria!

After only a second or so of these whirling thoughts, Annie started to come out of her hiding-place, to urge the girls back to the hatch. Gina saw her, but before Annie could say anything in warning, the two thieves burst out of the hole in the wall, carrying a large canvas.

Annie just managed to duck back behind the door, without being spotted. The men's eyes of course were drawn to the other girls, standing there at the entrance to the side passage.

'Gina!' cried Señor Bernabo, in surprise.

'What the hell are they doing here?' growled the Englishman.

Bernabo let fly a stream of Spanish. Annie heard him go over to Gina.

'Tie them up,' said the Englishman, joining him.

'We'll leave them down here,' said Señor Bernabo.

'It's too risky,' said the other. 'They can identify us both.'

'No, Gina is my niece. By the time they're found, we'll be out of the country.' said Bernabo. 'Come on!'

As the argument went on, Annie sent up a silent prayer that no harm would come to Gina or Maria. She hoped Sam had called the police and that he had been believed. At least the argument between the two crooks was gaining a little time.

With the girls' fate still in the balance, they were tied up and gagged. Muffled sobbing reached Annie's straining ears.

Suddenly another, much more welcome, sound reached Annie's ears. The hatch was being opened. It must be the police!

The crooks heard it too.

'Someone's coming down!' said the Englishman.

'Let's go,' said Bernabo.

'No, they're too close, and these two would slow us down.'

'Leave them and run for it!' cried Bernabo. His voice sounded quaky.

As Annie listened intently, the blood pounding in her head, she heard only one set of footsteps coming down the steps. Not the police then!

With horror, she guessed it must be Sam, alone. About to be confronted by two dangerous men.

She saw Bernabo and his accomplice slipping down the passageway, probably preparing to pounce on Sam.

Forgetting her own danger, she jumped out from behind the door and yelled a warning to him. The men shouted in surprise as Pip and Cherry, too, came out of their hiding-place.

The next second there was a blinding flash. Annie guessed Sam must have used his camera.

Annie knew she had to act now, while the crooks were temporarily dazzled.

She shouted to Pip and Cherry to follow her.

'The door!' she yelled.

They looked aghast at her. They could see what she was intending – to pull the door shut on the crooks – but they hadn't been able to budge it at all earlier.

They each called upon their best reserves of strength, and, aided by Sam, who had quickly guessed what they were up to, they heaved the oak door shut.

They thanked heaven for the thick oak of that door! It was an excellent barrier between themselves and the crooks. While the girls held on tightly to the knob, Sam released Gina and Maria from their bonds.

'Ready to run?' Annie asked her friends. The two men were rattling and pulling at the knob on the other side of the door. She again had doubts as to whether the children would manage to get to the hatch in time.

But at that point, the police arrived in force. They streamed down the steps and soon had the situation under control. The children stood away from the door, while they opened it and arrested the thieves.

'What on earth are you children doing down here?' demanded the policeman in charge. 'I'm Inspector Dash,' he went on. 'I think you've got a little explaining to do.'

While Annie wondered where on earth to begin, he picked up the painting which the men had been holding.

'The Degas!' he said. 'Your friend was right.'

As four of his constables led the men past him, his tone softened a little. 'Are any of you hurt?'

Two women constables were already talking to Gina and Maria. When all the children had assured him they were fine, the Inspector smiled.

'So, we have the Dance Club to thank for catching our art-thieves,' he said. 'It's a good job we believed your friend, here.'

He paused, and looked at Sam.

'I fear you were running a considerable risk in tackling these men,' he said. 'Who are they anyway, do you know?'

'One is my uncle,' said Gina, unflinchingly. 'Señor Bernabo.' She stood with her chin up as she said it.

'But Gina knew nothing about what he was up

to,' Annie said hastily. 'She didn't even know what *we* were suspecting. She and Maria stumbled in here by accident.'

'I see,' said Inspector Dash, 'so the rest of you guessed there was going to be a break-in?'

'Sort of,' said Annie, 'but we didn't know when. Our main reason for coming down here was just to explore the secret tunnel.'

'And the other man?'

When Annie had given him the dealer's name, the Inspector looked surprised. 'He's a reputable antiques dealer,' he said.

One of the women PCs approached him. 'I think we'd better call an ambulance, sir,' she said. 'These two girls were tied and gagged apparently. They might be suffering from shock.'

Maria, who had been very quiet indeed, seemed to agree to this suggestion.

But Gina shook her head vehemently. 'I have a show this afternoon. I not miss. I am the star!'

Inspector Dash looked at her in surprise.

'Well,' he said, 'if you're sure you're all right. What about the rest of you? Anyone want to be taken straight home?'

There was a chorus of 'nos'.

'Tough bunch, aren't they?' he said to the woman PC. 'I expected to be taking you all back to the station to make statements …'

He looked at their crestfallen faces. 'But it can wait until after the performance.'

'I'll take Maria up to the entrance, sir,' said the

woman PC. 'We can watch for the ambulance.'

'Are you OK, Maria?' Gina asked her in a concerned tone. 'I'm sorry I got you into this.'

'I've never been so terrified in all my life,' said Maria, finding her voice. 'If I'd known your uncle was a *criminal* ...'

She didn't finish her sentence before being led away, but it was pretty obvious she wanted nothing more to do with Gina.

Annie put her arm round Gina, as she looked upset. 'You've still lots of friends in the club,' she said. 'Me, for one!'

'Thank you, Annie,' Gina said.

The friends were taken up to the café on the ground floor, and given hot, sweet cups of tea. Annie's throat was parched and she drank it down quickly.

'That better?' the inspector said. 'Could you stand answering a few more questions?'

While the girls told him the whole story, one of the constables went off to find Mr Farr and Mrs Race. The teachers looked terribly shocked when they arrived in the café, but were reassured once they had spoken to their five young pupils.

'We'd better cancel your dance display,' said Mr Farr.

'Oh, no!' cried Annie. 'We are all fit to dance. We wouldn't miss it for the world.'

When Gina had added her own plea, Mr Farr saw it was useless to argue.

'You don't look much like dancers at the

moment,' said Mrs Race. 'You'd better go and have a good wash. At least you'll have clean costumes to put on!'

'Before you rush off, can I just ask you for the film from your camera, young man?' said Inspector Dash. 'It might have an important piece of evidence on it.'

'Oh right – the flash photo I took of the men!' said Sam.

'It's not every day we get them photographed red-handed,' said the Inspector. 'Nice work!'

Sam handed over the film and went off, walking ten feet tall.

The girls had a shock when they saw their grimy faces, grey hair and filthy clothes in the mirror of the cloakroom. Mrs Race had found some squirty soap and proper towels from somewhere, so they were able to wash their hair in the sinks as well as their faces, necks and hands.

In the dressing-room, their other friends crowded round them, and they had to repeat the story once again. Clemmie had popped in to check on the costumes, and was horrified when she heard the full adventure.

'I'm so glad none of you were hurt,' she whispered. She clasped Annie's hand. 'You really shouldn't do such dangerous things!'

Annie smiled to herself. She could almost hear Clemmie's mother speaking through her.

'Well, I must say, I was pretty frightened,' said Annie.

137

'I bet,' said Robbie. 'But you were so brave, coming out to shout that warning to Sam!'

Annie beamed with pleasure.

'And Sam so brave, too,' Toni piped up.

But Robbie wouldn't be diverted: he went on chatting to Annie, asking her all sorts of questions about their underground ordeal.

Cherry had to interrupt the conversation, to remind them they'd better start getting changed into their 'Little Match Girl' costumes.

'It's a good job you're not dancing till later, Gina,' said Annie. Gina was beginning to look rather peaky. 'You're sure you're going to be able to cope?'

'Si,' said Gina. 'I will dance!'

'Let's go and find a seat outside,' suggested Clemmie. 'We can watch the ballet. A bit of fresh air and a rest will probably do you good.'

As Gina went off with Clemmie and Toni, Annie felt she would be in good hands. She could now put her mind on the dancing which lay ahead.

As she got changed, she uncovered the grazes and bruises on her left shoulder and leg. One of the ducklings offered her a tube of antiseptic cream. This soothed the sore places, and Annie put some thick foundation on the top of it, to disguise the bruises.

In no time at all she was transformed into a sleek, clean-looking angel. Her Dance Club friends behind her, she led the way through the castle and into the grounds.

Mr Farr had set up a sound system beside the stage and was standing by to put on their tapes. As Susie mounted the stage, dressed as the Little Match Girl, Annie spotted her own parents and sister taking their seats.

If only they knew what I've just been through, she thought to herself.

'The Little Match Girl' went like a dream. All the club members knew it so well now that they could relax and do their very best. Susie gave a beautiful performance as the Match Girl and Annie knew she had danced very well herself in her role as Chief Angel.

As the company took their bows, Annie caught sight of several members of the audience wiping their eyes. She felt a terrific thrill that her ballet had moved even a few people that much!

And then it was back to the dressing-room. Surrounded by small girls from the marching troupe, they frantically discarded their costumes, and pulled on their sequin-decorated unitards. Gina of course had had more time to get ready.

'Are you sure you're all right?' Annie asked her.

'I am fine,' said Gina.

They went out to the arena together, the others following in an orderly way. There were gasps of admiration for the costumes from the audience, as the members of the Dance Club entered the ring. Annie just hoped Clemmie could hear them.

Annie stopped worrying about Gina. Her face glowing, Gina performed the difficult sequence of acrobatic dancing with amazing ease. In fact everyone managed the challenging choreography of 'Squib' very well. They even managed to hold their 'human pyramid' at the end for a record six seconds. Gina was balanced at the very top, standing on Annie's and Pip's shoulders (they were on the second tier). Just before they all jumped down, Gina let go of their hands and held her own arms high.

The crowd roared with delight. The Dance Club had never had such applause before! It seemed to go on for ever! Annie spotted Mr Rodding in the crowd, with little Timmy perched on his shoulders, waving wildly.

As they bowed once more to the cheering crowd, Annie reflected on all the obstacles they had had to get over, to put on their show at the castle.

It was all well worth it, though, she decided. And on the way, they had unmasked Señor Bernabo and the antiques dealer for the criminals they were!

She took Gina's hand, gave it a squeeze, then stepped forward with her, presenting her to the audience. For the first time, Annie felt not the slightest pang of envy. Gina deserved her applause.

She looked round at her friends and grinned at them. They grinned back. The Dance Club was turning out to be just as exciting as Annie had always promised it would.

For Juliet and Dan Conway
and Sarah Peck

DANCE CLUB 1

FOOTPRINT IN THE CLAY

It's just the beginning for the Dance Club

Annie's friends love her idea of forming a dance club in school, and it's not long before they're putting together a show. However, the Dance Club has its fair share of problems – tension and rivalry between members threaten the club's survival, and then they find themselves being suspected of burglary …

DANCE CLUB 2

DOUBLE TROUBLE

Trouble for the Dorricott twins

Not only are Kim and Susie behaving
strangely, but Pip gets a nasty letter, and then
Annie is suddenly ignored by all her Dance
Club friends. There's also the Salop Dance
Festival to rehearse for. Can the Dance Club's
entry make the grade?

DANCE CLUB 3

SKELETON IN THE WARDROBE

Ghostly happenings
at the dance studio

The Rodelle School of Dance is to put on its first show at Easter and Annie and Cherry are thrilled to have solo parts. But there are strange goings on at the school. Annie is convinced a ghost is haunting the building – what other explanation could there be for the eerie wailing they can hear? Then they find a skeleton in the costume room …

DANCE CLUB 5

FLOWERS AND FIREWORKS

Conflict and drama for the Dance Club

The Dance Club are in trouble when Mrs Sampson, the fierce new PE teacher, bans them from using the gym. The pressure is also on Cherry when her sporting and dancing commitments clash. But when the Dance Club are asked to perform at the Shrewsbury Flower Show, the fireworks really start to fly.

DANCE CLUB 6

SUMMER SCHOOL SECRETS

*There's more than one secret
to be kept at Summer School*

The Dance Club are thrilled to be at Dame
Kiritova's Summer School by the sea. But
there's strong competition for the prestigious
dancing scholarships to be awarded at the
end of the course. Then Sam notices strange
activity in the caves below the school,
and the Dance Club find themselves in
serious danger …